ALBERT

by

DON MILLER

Author of the Award-Winning Novel,
Lamb's Creek

Dog Pound Press

ALBERT
Dog Pound Press Paperback Edition / September 2017

For information contact Dog Pound Press at
www.DonMillerWriter.com

Dog Pound Press
ISBN-10: 0-9971061-1-4
ISBN-13: 978-0-9971061-1-4

ALBERT was written by Don Miller with advice and review provided by Paula Miller and Cindy Taylor

Edited by Alvin Guy, alvineguy@yahoo.com

Cover design and graphics by MillerLine Design

Author Photo by Webster Miller, Copyright © 2011

TO MY FAMILY

CHAPTER ONE

In the huge foyer opening into his private office, Lord Albert Anderson stood gazing at the long line of paintings of his ancestors hanging on the walls. Every one of them had served England in the past and served well. Lord Albert Anderson had done the same. He fought in Africa, spent four years in India and had held high-ranking offices in Parliament. He also had been knighted for his outstanding service, something only one other of his forefathers had attained. He made a mental note that he must soon have a painting of himself placed at the end of the line.

This in turn reminded him today was his birthday. *Seventy years old and where have all the years gone? If only I could recall just a few of those years I would not need to have this meeting with my grandson, but it is something which must be taken care of. I have put it off too long already and should have tended to it months ago*; he chided himself again for his procrastination. Lord Anderson turned and entered his office. The furnishings were elaborate. He could not remember how many generations had used it without changing or replacing anything. A portrait of his deceased wife was the only addition he had made to the office. It had been hanging in her bedroom ever since the French artist painted it six years ago, two years before her untimely death. The doctors said she died from internal infections. After her death, he moved the portrait into his office so he could see her every day. *Oh, Eleanor, why didn't I listen to you and retire back then? We could have had a couple of years together. The things I thought so important now seem utterly futile.*

Lord Anderson stood erect, as straight as when he was twenty years old. The thing that gave his age away was his hair, white as snow, though not a hair was missing. It was a trait of his family; none of the men were bald. He was looking out the eight-foot-tall window at the well-kept lawns and pastures beyond, hating what he now had to do.

The family fortunes were great. Lord Anderson himself did not know the extent of his investments, which had been inherited nor of those that he had since acquired. All he knew was he was getting old and must make some kind of arrangements for his vast holdings. His only son surely could not be trusted to manage such an empire. Phillip could not even stand up to his conniving wife, who had ruined him financially and could not wait to get her hands on the Anderson fortunes. Their son though, with a little help, may be what he was looking for. Albert should be coming in sight any moment now.

****

It was seven o'clock in the morning when Lady Abigail went into her son's room to awaken him. He had just gotten to bed three hours before after a night of carousing. She called his name and he never moved. She gently scratched his back and mussed his curly black hair, nothing. "You are supposed to have a meeting with your grandfather this morning, Albert." He jumped out of bed with a wild look in his eyes. "What time is it, Mother?"

"Don't worry, Son. You have plenty of time. It is only seven o'clock."

Albert's meeting with his grandfather was at nine and he knew he was expected to be there at that time, not one minute later.

"What does the old geezer want you for, Son?"

"I don't know, Mother, and I don't like you calling him names. He has always been kind to us and we should respect him for it."

There are ways to find out what he is up to, she thought. *I'll know before this day is over.*

Albert hurriedly dressed and went to the stables to saddle his dappled gray horse. Dap was a gift from Lord Anderson on his sixteenth birthday. This was five years ago and hardly a day passed when he had not ridden him except the times he was away at school. As usual, Dap was waiting for Albert to come from the house. The large house and stables were a part of his grandfather's estate located one mile from the castle where he now lived. Two years ago, Lord Anderson decided to retire and since then, he rarely traveled to London. In the last year, Albert had visited with his grandfather several times and come to realize he was a gentle man and not at all like his mother had led him to believe. Albert had not known a lot about him and very seldom talked to him until he retired and moved back home.

"I wonder what he does want, Dap?" Albert asked as he headed for the castle.

The early morning air was crisp and Dap wanted to control the gait. He wanted to stretch out, though Albert had too much on his mind this morning. Usually he would let his horse run until he slowed of his own accord but not this morning. "Wait until after we talk with Grandfather, boy, then you can run to your heart's content."

When he turned into the road lined with two hundred-year-old elm trees overlapping the drive, he looked at his gold pocket watch. It was eight forty-five. Albert decided he was ten minutes early and this would be as bad as being late. He pulled on the reigns slightly and Dap started prancing. "Good boy! You must think someone is watching to show off like this."

Someone was. Lord Anderson had seen his grandson prancing his horse and watched him until he turned to go to the stables behind the house. He looked at his timepiece and it showed five minutes to nine. *Punctuality is one thing I like about Albert. He is never late. I wonder though, if after he hears what I have to say, will I ever see him again?* While he was still pondering this, Margaret, his wife's longtime companion and close friend knocked on the door of his office and announced he had a guest. Albert entered and said with his big smile. "Good morning, Grandfather." Lord Anderson simply nodded and asked how was he getting along. He wanted to get started with what was to him serious business, and he so much as said so.

As Lord Anderson motioned for his grandson to sit, he noticed the door had not been closed completely. He almost had to smile, but did not. *Just as I thought, Margaret is on the job. Our Lady Abigail will hear the news shortly.*

"Albert, what I have to say is strictly between you and me, and I want to keep it this way." Albert nodded his head he understood. "I think it is time you do something with your life. Too much spare time is not good for a young man of your age. I want you to join the military and I will arrange for you to receive a commission in the Royal Army. If you agree to this, you will be paid handsomely and your mother will also reap many benefits. You can have one week to make a decision. If your answer is no, you and your mother will be cut from my will. Now, this is such a pretty day what say we go and exercise our horses." Albert could not believe what his grandfather just said. It did not make any sense at all. Could he have lost his mind? Lord Anderson was immediately walking towards the door while motioning for Albert to follow.

Silence walked with the two heading for the stables. Albert had always thought his grandfather to be in complete control of his faculties.

The stable hand wasted no time in getting the horses ready to go and the two riders walked their horses towards the top of the highest hill in the area, a place they called The Knob. Albert always liked to go there because one could see for miles in any direction. Lord Anderson did not stop when they reached the top but continued on.

"I have to make sure of what I think is going on, Son, bear with me." The older man dismounted and told Albert to come with him. They ground hitched their horses and eased back up the hill. Hardly a minute passed until someone left the castle and went to the stables. "Your eyes are better than mine. Who do you make it out to be?" he asked his grandson.

"Miss Margaret, sir. What is going on?"

"Let's wait just one minute and see where she goes. If I am right, she will go and see your mother."

"What will all this prove and why all the suspense?"

"I'll try and explain later, be patient."

Sure enough, Margaret drove the buggy to where Albert and his mother lived, got out and almost ran to the house. The door opened before she could knock and someone pulled her in.

"Just what I expected. Now there is no doubt in my mind whatsoever, the spy has revealed herself."

Albert was still unsure of what was going on. He had a puzzled look and asked, "What?"

"I will explain as best I can. Your mother has known for the last two years what has been going on in my life. Where I go, most everything I do, what my private conversations are and everything else. Now I understand how. What I said while in my office was not for your ears but your mother's. I am sorry you had to find out this way, Son, but now we both know."

"Why are they doing this, and what do they hope to accomplish?"

"Who really knows what goes on in a person's mind? Margaret hates me because she thinks I should have spent more time with your grandmother, and she is right. I should have. Your mother sees me as someone who is standing in her way to a great fortune, a fortune that she will never get. You don't understand yet, do you?"

"To me all I see is two conniving women, Grandfather, and I agree with you, they don't like you."

"Enough said about what went on this morning. I would like to know about your life goals. What are your plans for the future? Tell me your dreams, Albert."

These questions coming from his grandfather surprised him. Such an important man wanting to know about him, indeed this was something.

Albert tried to remember all of the questions he was asked. *Goals: I have none,* he thought. *Future plans: the same answer. Dreams: none. What is he getting at?* "Sir, I don't understand what you're asking me."

"Are you telling me you have never thought about what you want in life?"

Albert was getting a little flustered, being asked such personal questions.

"Mother wants me to marry Jane Abbot."

"Why?"

"Her father has a lot of money I suppose is the reason."

"Do you want to marry Jane? Do you love this Jane?"

"I don't know the answers to either of those questions, Grandfather. Is it so important at this time in my life?"

Lord Anderson was beginning to show his impatience. "Albert Anderson, are you telling me you would marry someone you can't say you love because your mother says her father has a lot of money? Do you know how long a marriage like this will last? No time at all. I had a lot of hope for you, but now I see that maybe this hope is in vain. You best go and think about what was said here today. Come and see me one week from today at the same time and we will talk again. If you don't have any more answers than you have now, don't show up."

Both men, one seventy and the other only twenty-one years of age, mounted their horses and walked them slowly down the hill to the stables without saying a word. When they dismounted, Albert nodded his head to his grandfather who did not acknowledge his nod but quickly headed for his castle.

Entering his office, he closed and locked the door. He paused in front of Eleanor's portrait.

"I need advice, darling. What would you do about this? I don't even have patience with our own grandson. Please show me what to do." He sat in his soft cushioned chair and for the first time in his life he really did not know what to do.

Give it time, Albert, give it time.

Lord Albert Anderson was asleep and thought he was dreaming.

****

Dap seemed to know something was wrong with his master. Normally, he would want to run as fast as he could, though not now. Albert was in a quandary about the visit with his grandfather. *I'm a grown man and I know there are some things expected of me. What things, and how am I to know what to do? Why would he expect these things of me?*

His head was jammed with questions when he entered his house.

"What did the Lord want of you, Albert?" The question caught him off guard and it took him a second to regain his senses.

"Nothing really, Mother. Please excuse me I have things I have to do."

All that afternoon, Albert sat in his bedroom and pondered what was discussed that morning. *Did Grandfather want something more of me than what we talked about? I feel I must have missed something which was very important to him. He made me feel like I was a kid, really intimidated. Do I act like a kid? Am I not responsible?* To these questions, he had no answers.

That evening his mother brought some soup and crackers to his room. He wanted to ask her about Miss Margaret's visit then decided to wait until she brought it up. *If Grandfather is right, she will*. He no more than thought of it when she asked.

"You are going to enlist in the Royal Army, aren't you, Son?"

He thought of several ways to answer her but could not bring himself to speak to her in such a way.

"Mother, I'm not hungry and I have a lot of thinking to do. I will let you know when I make a decision."

"I don't want to influence you, Albert, but you should do what he wants you to do. It will mean a lot to me and you will not have to marry what's her name. Just say you will think on it. Are you sure you don't want to eat?"

"I'm sure, Mother, thank you."

After his mother left, Albert became angry. *So, Grandfather was right. She uses people as pawns. She manipulates whomever she can to get what she wants. Why could I not see this before? What about Father, what has she done to him?*

After a while he began to calm down. *Grandfather, thank you, thank you for making me see what I should have already seen. I do need to grow up and I have a lot of things to think about, but now I am tired and I'm going to bed.* That night Albert slept like a log.

The next morning, he was up early wanting to ride his horse. Having not eaten the evening before, he was famished. He dressed in riding clothes and made his way to the kitchen hoping not to see anyone. The sun had not come up yet but there was someone in the kitchen preparing breakfast. It was Alma, the new girl they had employed only one month ago.

When Albert entered the kitchen, it caught her off guard and she let out a little squeal.

"Sorry, I didn't mean to frighten you," Albert said. "I didn't know anyone would be up so early."

She composed herself quickly. "Quite alright, sir. I couldn't sleep so decided to get things ready for when Miss Morgan is ready to fix breakfast. Can I do something for you this morning?"

"Just a cup of tea and a muffin or toast will be fine if you have it. I am in sort of a hurry. I have been neglecting my horse lately and it looks to be a fine day for riding."

Albert sat at the kitchen table as Alma prepared his food. He had seen her a time or two, but until now, had not noticed how attractive she was.

He gulped his tea and muffin and thanked her as he hurried for the stables. No one was around so he saddled Dap himself. "We didn't get that ride I promised you yesterday ol' boy, so today we will do double if you are up to it." Dap was up to it and they left the stable yard at a run and did not bother going through the gate. Over the stone fence he went clearing the top by two feet. "Wow, you surely are in a mood this morning, Dap. You just do your thing and I will see if I can hang on." Two miles had passed before they began to slow. It was another crisp morning and the two, both horse and rider, were in top shape and seemed ready to take on the world.

"I say we go check out the outcropping ol' boy, it's been a while since we were there." The place covered almost one-quarter mile with boulders of all sizes, which looked like they had been hand placed. Albert had played there often when he was younger and knew all the places one could hide. He slipped the bridle off his horse so he could eat the lush grass while

Albert climbed around on the boulders. *Those were fun days he recalled, when I was a kid. But I am not a kid. I am a grown man and not a child any longer. Is this what Grandfather wanted me to understand? And what about Mother and Father, especially Father?* He was beginning to understand his mother and did not like how she used people. He realized he knew nothing about his father except what he was told; he was a sick man and had to stay in a special place for his kind of sickness. He remembered when he was very small, he went with his mother to see him, though he remembered hardly anything. He was told his father could not see them again and no one ever talked about him anymore. Albert had a compelling desire to see his father and decided when he met with his grandfather again, he would ask him to go with him for a visit.

They took the long way back to the castle detouring by way of The Knob where the conversation took place the day before. Albert dismounted and looked around at the vast surroundings. All of this belonged to his grandfather, and then it hit him. *He was trying to feel me out, to see if I was the one he could count on to be responsible for his vast empire. How blind can one be? It had never dawned on me that some day...* He stopped there not wanting to go any further. *This is what has been on his mind probably for a long time. Good Lord. There is no way I would know what to do. This is what Mother has on her mind also; she wants to inherit all of Grandfather's wealth. I feel like him; never, never, never.* All of this was too much for Albert to grasp. He stood and looked at the castle where he knew his grandfather was. Maybe he was looking at him now. Albert waved both his arms and then thought, odds are, he does not even know I am out here today. He loped Dap down the hill and through the gate to the stables.

Lord Albert Anderson was waiting for him.

"Did you see me waving from The Knob?" he asked excitedly.

"I did, and I knew you would be here shortly. If I had known you were riding today I would have joined you. It is such a fine day just to be alive."

Albert handed Dap over to the stable hand. "About yesterday, I am sorry, sir, for the way I acted. I was not ready for your questions and didn't have a clue as to what you were talking about."

"And now, what do you suppose I was talking about?"

Albert did not know where to start; he started to say something and stopped. He lifted his hands and pointed in each direction. "It's about this, your land, your castle, all of your holdings. These things have never crossed my mind, Grandfather, and I am so sorry. I have always taken you for granted, that you would always be here and able to care for everything by yourself. All I ever thought about is myself. Am I right?"

"Close, Son, close. I am not thinking about cashing in just now, though my age is finally catching up with me, and there is no one I can trust to carry on when I can no longer tend to everything. Tell me, what made you think of what you just said?"

"I have thought of nothing but of what you said since yesterday. This morning while riding, things just came together. I saw all of this property and asked myself, who is going to take care of Grandfather and his investments when he is no longer able? Father would be next in line but I haven't seen him since I was six years old. Before we talk about anything else, I want you to tell me about my father. Mother forbids me to even mention him. I have to know and I want you to take me to see him."

Lord Anderson was astonished at hearing this. Though he would not have mentioned it, he had been thinking a lot about Phillip lately. Lady Eleanor would want him to do this. She had gone to see him on the first day of every month since she admitted him to a private hospital that cared for people with psychological disorders.

"Albert, this is a hard thing you ask of me. I will try and explain as best I can. Your father has mental problems. As a young child, he could not deal with any kind of stress. He would just curl up into a ball if he were confronted with any little matter. My wife, bless her, tended to him. Phillip would have nothing to do with me. He wouldn't speak if I were in his presence. As he got older he seemed a little better. When he met your mother, he was in his mid-thirties and she had a way with him that not even Eleanor had. He wanted permission to marry her and this pleased his mother so. Two years later, you were born and that was when things began to change. He started to drink heavily and to revert back to his earlier years. Your mother badgered him to ask for more of his inheritance and when he would not, she came to me and demanded what he would not ask for.

She had spent every cent he had trying to impress society minded people, something she could never do. They saw right through her. Your father could not cope with her and went into a worse state than before. Finally, my wife asked if I would permit her to have him admitted to the hospital where he is today. I haven't been to see him since then, and this shames me. I used the excuse it may make him worse if I did. I cannot tell you any more than that, and yes, I will take you whenever you want to go. It is time for me to see my son and for you to meet your father. Now, no, tomorrow, if you can, let's go tomorrow. I have a few things I need to attend to this evening."

It was agreed upon, they would leave first thing in the morning.

CHAPTER TWO

Lord Anderson had much on his mind as he strolled the short distance to the castle. He went straight to his office and closed the door. He could not believe how much difference one day could make in people's lives. "Eleanor, yesterday I didn't think our grandson would ever amount to a hill of beans. Today, I believe he could probably do anything he set his mind to. You know what he wants? He wants to go see his father, and you know what? I want to see our son. Tomorrow we are going to do just that."

****

Albert rode the mile to his home in record time; he also had a lot on his mind. He unsaddled Dap, rubbed him down and gave him a bucket of oats. His mother saw him enter the stable yard and was waiting for him.

"You had me worried, Son. You never leave without letting me know."

"I have had a lot to think about, Mother. I left before anyone was up and I seem to be able to think better riding in the countryside."

"Have you considered what your grandfather wants you to do? I'm not telling you what to do, Albert, but it would mean much to me if you complied with his wishes."

"No, Mother, the military is not for me. I am going to marry Jane."

Lady Abigail fainted. Albert caught her before she hit the floor and placed her on the divan. He fanned her until she began to move and open her eyes. "Son, you can't marry that girl."

"You yourself picked her for me, Mother. Your very words were 'her family is rich' and 'I would never have to worry about money'. Now, I have a lot to do but you don't have to think about the wedding. It is already taken care of. I am going to London in the morning to buy a whole new wardrobe."

"What about me? What will happen to me?"

"We'll talk about this when I get back," Albert said as he ran up the stairs.

It was still dark when Albert rode Dap into the castle stables with his two handbags. The driver was hitching the white horses to the beautiful coach. Even in the lamplight, one could see the coach was not ordinary; it was a deep dark red and black with gold leaf trimming. The inside was cushioned and padded. The windows had red velvet curtains that could be closed for privacy. Albert placed his bags in the storage compartment and then led Dap to his stable. "I'll be back in a few days ol' boy, and we'll do some more riding."

Lord Anderson, along with a servant carrying his bags, arrived. He motioned for the driver to join them. "I do not want either of you to tell anyone where we are. There will be questions I am sure, but you are to say nothing." Both agreed to his demand. They arrived at the little train station as it was getting light. No other passengers boarded the train. The conductor knew Lord Anderson and led them to a private car. The train began to lurch forward and the two men sat in their seats facing each other. There was a small table between the seats and Lord Anderson placed his top hat on it. In their conversation, Albert related his story about what he told his mother. When he got to the part where she fainted, Lord Anderson threw back his head and laughed uncontrollable, bumping his silver tipped ebony cane on the floor. He hardly ever allowed himself to smile let alone to laugh out loud.

The train ride took only four hours. A hotel carriage was waiting for the passengers and took them straight to the luxurious, three-story hotel. Everyone knew Lord Anderson and they were soon escorted to the large room he usually occupied when in London. It was still early when they decided to go to the hospital. A twenty-minute ride brought them to a large old building in pristine condition. A six-foot wrought iron fence enclosed the building and the large immaculate lawns and flower gardens. A well-dressed butler received them and seated them in a comfortable waiting room. In a couple of minutes Dr. Carberry entered and introduced himself, knowing immediately who his guests were.

"We have been expecting you, Lord Anderson, and this must be Sir Albert. There is a wonderful surprise awaiting you. I would like to talk to you before you see your son. You will not know Sir Phillip. As far as we can tell, he is completely well and has been dismissed as a patient for at least a year. We offered to take him home but he said he was going to wait for you to come and get him. He has been working on staff here for a length of time. He is one of the best with the other patients because of what he went through. He can relate to them and, therefore, do more than any other of our staff. Now, if you will wait for a few minutes, I will send someone to tell him his father and son want to see him."

Neither one could believe what they just heard. They looked dumbfounded at each other.

"Sir, did he just say Father was waiting for us to come and get him? How did he know we would?"

"I can't understand any of what he said."

A distinguished looking middle-aged man with white hair wearing a white doctor's smock entered the room and went directly up to Lord Anderson.

"Father, I am your son, Phillip. I knew when the time was right, you would come." He shook his father's hand, and then looked at Albert.

"And you must be my son, Albert." He likewise shook his hand. "I understand what you must be feeling. Let's sit and get reacquainted. It has been quite a long time since we saw each other and under much different circumstances."

It took a minute for the two men to regain their composure and to accept what was going on. Never would they have guessed Phillip would be like this - a well man in charge of all his faculties. They could not believe it. He told them he had a hard time accepting his mother's death and it was almost more than he could handle, but knew it must have been hard on others also.

Lord Anderson did not know how to deal with this altogether new situation so he asked Phillip what his plans were. "Dr. Carberry said you had a position here. Is this what you want to do?"

"I have seriously considered working here and I may, though I would like to visit with you and get to know my son. Would it be alright if we tried it out to see what happens?"

"There is nothing I would rather do, Son, than have you home again. Do you want to go back to live with your wife and

Albert?"

He smiled and asked his father if he was joking. "She is no longer my wife and hasn't been for fifteen years. The last time she was here she wanted a divorce and had the papers and you can bet I signed them without asking a question. This was the last time I saw you, Albert. I believe you were six years old."

This was something else that was unknown to them.

"Father, no one knew about any of this until now. I am sorry we have lost all these years. I, for one, am looking forward to us being together. This is the best thing ever to happen."

Two hours later, Phillip was ready to go and he had the hospital carriage take them back to the hotel.

"We will have a feast and celebrate your homecoming, Son," Lord Anderson informed them when they entered their hotel room. "The best place in London to eat is just two blocks from here. I have indulged myself there many times."

The three generations of Andersons, dressed in their finest clothes, walked to George's Dining. The restaurant was known for its quality steaks. When they entered, the owner himself, knowing Lord Anderson, brought them to a private dining room and sent the chief chef to take their order.

"What a meal," Albert commented when he took the last bite. "I have to admit, that was the best steak I have ever eaten."

The day was coming to a close when they entered their hotel room.

"We will get a good night sleep and leave for home in the morning if this will be to your satisfaction," Lord Albert said. "I am beginning to feel my years on days like this."

Before he went to sleep, Lord Anderson thanked God for all the things that had happened the last two days. He had formed a relationship with his grandson and, what his darling wife had always wanted, regained their son who now seemed to be as normal as could be.

****

For the last year, Phillip had a longing to be with his son, whom he had not seen for fifteen years, and also his father, if he was still alive. Now he would be put to the test and hoped that all would go well. *I do so want to be a part of my family and for them to be able to count on me.* Since his mother's death, he had been applying himself to studying. Not only for the hospital but also in accounting and business management. This had helped him keep his mind off his problems. The university was in walking distance from the hospital and he had gone there three days a week and regarded himself a part of society. *Time will tell*, he thought as he closed his eyes.

****

What would have happened to me if Grandfather had not talked to me the other day? Albert thought as he prepared for bed. *He sure had me going in circles for a couple of days. I had never thought about being a part of his empire or anything else. Me was all that mattered. That is the way Mother is and I must say, it is not very becoming. If he had not talked to me the way he did, none of this would have happened. Grandfather would have to look outside the family for help, I would never have known Father, and what would I have turned out to be, a nothing, a parasite? Thank you, Lord, for both my father and grandfather and help me to know what to do.*

At seven o'clock the next morning when the train left

London, the three Anderson men were already on board. In their conversation, Lord Anderson asked Phillip basically the same questions he had asked Albert. What were his goals and what did he want in life?

"At this time, I really don't know." He shared with them that he had gone to the university and majored in accounting and business management.

This information really got his father's attention and he began to question Phillip more thoroughly.

"This is turning out to be very interesting," he said. "When we get home, we must sit together and discuss matters in greater detail. You may be just the one I am looking for."

Phillip was all ears, taking in every word his father said.

Lord Anderson turned to his grandson. "Albert, can you believe what has transpired from our discussion a few days ago? Now, we need to get back to you. What is it you want to do in life? If you don't have any goals, we ought to talk more about it. I can see you have a good mind and you must use it. Your life can be what you make it."

"Sir, this trip has taught me much. A week ago, I had nothing to interest me, and now there is so much I don't know what to do."

"You need most of all to grow up, Son, learn how to get along in the real world, and deal with real life experiences. When the time comes, you will know what it is you want. There is something I would like for you to do. I have been thinking about your mother and Miss Margaret. We cannot have them carrying on like they have been and I am going to let you decide what to do about it."

Phillip was told what the two women had been up to the last few years. How they eavesdropped on him and thought they had gotten away with it.

Albert said he had a plan and he would take care of the situation.

"I promised your grandmother I would take care of Margaret's finances as long as she lived but had I known, I don't think I could have made such a promise. It is in your hands now, see to it."

"If you will terminate Miss Margaret's job, sir, I will see that these two women live in the same house, together. Then we will see just how conniving they can be."

"I would rather them not know I am here, at least for a while," Phillip said.

"I do think that is a good idea. You stay in the cottage behind the barn when we get home, and I'll do as Albert says. I will give her notice and Albert can hurry her out with her stuff."

The plan was agreed upon and Albert was to handle the rest.

Lord Anderson hired a coach to bring them to his castle. They hurried Phillip through the barn and to the cottage. Albert and his grandfather went directly to the castle. Margaret met them at the door and seemed surprised to see them together.

"Margaret, come to my office, there is something I want to talk to you about, and, Albert, you come also."

The three marched in single file to Lord Anderson's office where he sat and motioned for them to sit.

"There has been a conspiracy going on between you and Abigail for years. I have known this for some time and now it is time I do something about it. I will not tolerate it any longer. I do not like doing things like this, Margaret, but you are no longer needed here. I promised my dear wife on her deathbed I would tend to your needs as long as possible, so you and your cousin Abigail can live together. You two will then have all the time you need to work out everyone's problems. You will leave immediately. Albert will help you move. This is all I have to say."

Lord Anderson stood up to leave and Margaret began to plead and said she was sorry; she would never do such things again. "I cannot live with that woman. She will drive me crazy, sir. If Lady Eleanor was alive, she would not want you to do this. Please let me stay here!"

"You should have thought of that before now, Margaret. I have made my decision and it will be carried out. Get your things together. Albert will take charge from now on."

He walked out leaving the bewildered woman, and with Albert feeling sorry for her.

"What have I done so bad to be treated like this? Tell me, Albert."

"Have you and Mother schemed against Grandfather in any way? Or is he making this up?"

"Well, we may have done some things, but not enough to warrant this."

"It won't be so bad living with Mother. It will be just you two. I am going to move here to be close to Grandfather. He is getting on in age and will need someone to help care for him. I will help you get your things together if you want."

Albert took her hand and led her to her room sobbing. The rest of the afternoon they packed and hauled her belongings to the large wagon and when the last piece was placed in the wagon, it was full. Albert helped her onto the seat beside him and they rode the mile in silence.

When they stopped the wagon in front of the house, Abigail ran out to see what was going on. "He just kicked me out, that's what, and for no good reason. Ask Albert, he was there."

"What are you talking about, who kicked you out and what are you doing here?"

"Mother, Grandfather knows what you and Miss Margaret have been doing. About you plotting and spying against him. Don't deny it. I have seen it also. You two will live here together and I am going to live at the castle for a while. Let's get these things into the house, then we will sit and talk, and you will know what is going on and why. No questions until then, please."

Lady Abigail was fuming all the while the wagon was being unloaded, not offering to lend a hand. Rodney, the stable boy, Miss Morgan, the cook, and Alma, the cook's helper, were called on to help with the unloading. After everything was placed in the room, Albert asked everyone to stay for a moment. They were all wondering what else was going to happen.

"Grandfather is making some changes in staff but none of you have to worry. You all will continue to have a job, though it may be at the castle. First, Rodney will be transferred to the castle. Alma will be transferred. Miss Morgan will stay here and continue to hold her position if she wants or Grandfather will give a letter of recommendation to her anytime she wishes. Rodney, you and Alma need to pack your belongings and be ready in the morning. Someone will be here to move you. If there are any questions, we will discuss them then. You are dismissed."

After they left, Albert faced the two women.

"Now, we will talk about us. What is it you want to know?"

"What in tarnation is going on here, Son? I thought you were getting married. What happened to change your mind?"

"Mother, please, you and Miss Margaret sit and I will try and explain this change. First, the wedding is not going to happen. Second, Grandfather and I went to London to see Father."

There was a gasp from his mother. "I told you never to mention him, Albert. I..."

Albert interrupted, "Mother, I'm a grown man and I will do as I wish. If you want to continue this talk, please be quiet."

"What has gotten in to you, Albert Anderson? You have never talked to me this way before. It's that Lord Grandfather of yours. I knew he would be your ruin."

Albert held up his hand to quiet his mother. "One more time and this conversation is over, is that clear?" His mother was fuming, though she said nothing more.

"Grandfather and I went to see my father. He was still at the hospital, though not a patient. He has a job there and is a doctor's assistant. Also, over the last few years, he has been to a university and has two degrees, one in accounting and one in business management. He is as sane as anybody and completely cured of his old illness. One more thing, Mother, he said you filed for a divorce fifteen years ago and he signed the papers. Why didn't you tell me about this?"

Abigail bowed her head but said nothing. Everything was coming down around her. She had regretted getting the divorce from Phillip and had tried to get it annulled but her lawyer said it would only be possible to annul it if Phillip agreed and signed the annulment papers within thirty days. She knew it was impossible because he had been too eager to sign the divorce papers. On top of that, now her son seemed to be against her. Not to mention her cousin is now living in the house with her. *Why is this all happening to me?*

Abigail was in deep thought when she realized Albert was still talking.

"The only help you will have will be Miss Morgan, your cook, if she agrees to stay here. You will be responsible for taking care of everything but the kitchen work. I know this seems completely absurd to you but it is all a result of your doing." Albert reached and took his mother's hand. "I truly am sorry to be the one to tell you this, please forgive me." He turned and walked out the door. The two women were dumbfounded and speechless.

Albert had never in his life spoken a harsh word to his mother or denied her anything she asked. He knew now she was the cause of his father having to be placed in the mental institution years ago, and she wanted him to marry someone wealthy so she would have use of their money. Still she was his mother and doing what he had done did not seem right. He entered the castle and as he walked past his grandfather's office, he was called to come in.

Both his father and grandfather were there and must have been for a while. Two empty cups and a tray with a few cookies were still on the desk. He tried to hide his downcast feelings from them but to no avail.

"I know this was a hard thing for you, Albert, and I am sorry you had to do it. You will find life will not consist of only good but also of hard and complicated decisions. Your mother and Margaret will learn to work out their problems as well as you. This is a big and difficult step you faced and I want you to know your father and I are proud of the way you handled it. Now if you care to join us, I will inform you what we have been discussing."

Before Albert came, Lord Anderson was explaining to Phillip his dilemma about finding someone capable of taking over the family holdings. He thought about Albert but found it was not possible, at this point, for him to manage such a huge empire.

Lord Anderson had said to Phillip, "The boy needs to get away from his mother and his so-called friends and find out what life is really about. In other words, he has to learn to be responsible for his actions. He didn't get the kind of upbringing he should have and I must say I am partly at fault."

"Albert, your father and I will be going back to London in a couple of days. I want to introduce him, and you also, to my good friend, Andy Smith, the gentleman who owns the law firm that handles all my legal work, and then to the financial agents who care for the investments. Tomorrow we will go over what property deeds and other documents I have here."

"Grandfather, what is it you think I should try and do? Things are so mind boggling to me right now."

"We were just talking about these things and I would like for you to think about what you want to do. I will tell you what I enjoyed most when I was your age, and that was the military. I went in refusing a commission and everyone thought I was crazy. It taught me to stand on my own two feet and grow up fast. With just six weeks of training, I was thrown into the thick of battle. The good Lord saw me through it and we overcame the enemy. After two years, I was as fit as everyone else and found life was what you make it. I am not telling you to do what I did; you will have to make such decisions for yourself. One has to do what he thinks best for himself and those around him."

The next day, Albert joined his father and grandfather as they examined all the legal papers in his safe at the castle, and this alone was worth a fortune.

"Grandfather, I don't want you to think I am not interested

in your estate and working with you and Father. I believe I am beginning to understand what you have been trying to tell me the last few days and I do need to find my own way. I ask you to excuse me from your London trip; there's a lot on my mind and I feel I must figure out some things. By the time, you two get back, I hope to know what I need to do."

Lord Anderson, though he did not say, thought this was a wise decision and stated it was acceptable.

CHAPTER THREE

The next morning Lord Anderson and his son, Phillip, entered his luxurious coach as Albert saddled Dap. "Ol' boy, I hope you're ready for a long day. We have a lot of ground to cover." The day before, while looking over the property maps of this place, he could hardly believe how huge it was. It was all fenced and Albert wanted to ride around the perimeter and get a feel for its size. He knew where two of the corners were and headed for the nearest one. What a fine day. The cool air and bright warm sun energized both he and Dap. The rolling hills slipped by as Dap galloped with his head held high. *What did Grandfather say the other day? 'It's good to be alive'?*

It took almost an hour to reach his starting place going at a gallop. The corner was marked with a massive column of hued gray stone. "We will follow the fence and see how long it takes to circle the property, Dap."

There were places where the under growth was so thick he had to leave the fence and go around for a ways. He had never seen this part before and was amazed at the size of the trees. Huge oak, maple, and beech, with other species he did not know. Three hours and he found the second corner was the same as the first. Some little ways further and he came to a small stream and dismounted to let Dap drink and rest before going on.

"What do you think you are doing?" an old gray-headed man shouted.

Albert did not know anyone was around. It caught him by surprise and startled him. "Just out for a ride." Was all he could think to say?

"You on private land, Sonny. How did you get on this side of my fence?"

Thinking he crossed over to someone else's property he answered, "Must have lost my way, sir. I was riding my grandfather's fence line and crossed by mistake. I will back track and see where I made my mistake." He started to mount Dap when the old man spoke again.

"Who be your grandpa, boy?"

"Lord Anderson, do you know him?"

"Come a little closer, my eyes don't see like they used to."

Albert walked the twenty feet to where the man was standing next to a fallen log and saw he was missing part of a leg from the knee down."

"You say your old man Anderson's grandson?"

Albert was caught off guard again. He had never heard anyone speak of his grandfather with disrespect before. "Lord Anderson is my grandfather, like I said."

"Sit down on this log awhile before I run you off. I've not heard another's voice in over a year. You don't know about me if I'm guessing right. People who know me think me crazy, but they're wrong. This land is rightfully mine. It belonged to my father before me and his father's back six generations. Good old England gave six square kilometers of land to your great grandfather and this land was included in that gift. I have a legal deed which says as far as a grown man can throw a rock three times in all four directions is the description of this piece of land. What galls me is, I'm the last of my line. I have no children and when I die, you will get it all. Now you talk so I can listen to someone besides myself."

This is an interesting old man, Albert thought. *Maybe I can get him to tell me about himself.* "I am Albert Anderson; may I ask who you are?"

"I am Beauregard Burton, but you can call me Bogie like everyone else. Your daddy must be crazy Phillip. Is he still in the insane asylum?"

"My father is completely well, thank you."

"Al, your grandpa and me are the same age. We use to play together as kids. We went to war at the same time; him to Africa and me to America. He received medals and me the loss of my leg. It was almost worth it though. That's where I would be now if I had two good legs. I would be climbing them Rocky Mountains and trapping beaver."

"Have you ever been to those mountains?"

"No, though I studied about America in school. Is it really four times as large as England?"

"Bigger, and they really have them wild Indians you read about."

Time was slipping away and Albert wanted to finish his ride before dark.

"I enjoyed our talk, Mr. Burton, but I have to go."

"I ain't quite ready to run you off yet. Can't you talk a little more?"

"Another time, and you can tell me more about America."

Albert left Bogie sitting on the log waving goodbye. The sun had gone down when he and Dap entered the stable yard. "Well, ol' boy, we are both wore out but we made the rounds and I never dreamed this place was so large."

35

The stable hand took Dap and Albert could not wait for a bath and something to eat. When he awoke the next morning, he went directly to his grandfather's office. He remembered seeing maps hanging on a rack and was hoping there might be one of America. Why was he excited? There was no reason for him to be. The third map proved to be what he sought - "The United States of America." This piece of land between Mexico and Canada was huge just like Mr. Burton said. He traced the Rocky Mountains with his finger from top to bottom. *Hundreds of miles*, he said to himself. *There is nothing like this here in England. I wonder what it really looks like, and is there really wild Indians? I doubt it, not in this day and age. I will ask Grandfather when he and Father gets back.*

Albert studied the map and noticed the eastern third of the country was where most of the towns and cities were, but nothing much in the western two thirds except along the Pacific coast.

There was a whole shelf in the study with information on America and he spent most of the day reading. He certainly knew about the revolution and the war between England and America, but what he learned in school was nothing compared to what was here. Stacks of news clippings his grandfather saved. Hundreds of soldiers lost their lives between 1775 and 1783, eight years of bloodshed. *These Americans must be really tough and aggressive people to fight a war so long to win their independence. I hope Grandfather comes back tomorrow; I need to talk to him.*

The next morning, Albert was back pouring over what new information he could find. *I cannot understand why I am so obsessed with this. What did that old man say, mountain men trapping beaver? What is so great about trapping beaver?*

He studied the map until he knew most of the larger cities and could name just about all the mountain ranges. Just before noon the hounds started barking, and when Albert looked, he saw his father and grandfather climbing out of the coach. Two servants had their luggage and were walking behind. Albert hurriedly put everything back in its place and went to welcome them home.

"How was the trip?" Albert asked.

"Long and tiresome, Son," his father answered. "Though I enjoyed every minute of it. I cannot thank my father enough for allowing me to be a working part of this family. There is so much I want to do. I feel like a little kid, a feeling I never felt before."

"Come, let us go and discuss with Albert the things we talked about on our ride back." Lord Anderson ordered tea and cake to be brought to his office and the three men went to await the refreshments.

"I believe your father is going to be the man I need to carry on this family's business, Albert. His schooling has prepared him for much of what it takes to manage our holdings. We still need to do a lot of planning and probably have to hire several qualified people to man an office. We are thinking about an office in London sometime in the near future, but for now we will work from here. What we want to know is if you would like to work with us."

"I will be glad to be a part of your team, Grandfather, though I don't think I am ready for such things. I have no schooling as Father, and to be truthful, I feel I would be more of a liability. If you will allow me a couple years to find out about myself and like you say, 'to grow up', I believe it would benefit all of us."

"Son, I know just how you feel," Phillip stated. "I experienced the same thing, though in a different way. You are right in wanting to be sure of something before taking it on." Phillip addressed his father, "Sir, I think it wise to let Albert have time to make his way for a while like you did. On his own, he will learn more than any other way. He cannot learn life experience behind a desk or in school."

Lord Anderson did not say anything for a minute. He refilled his cup with hot tea and walked to the tall window and stared at the beautiful landscape. He was thinking of when he was the age of Albert. *I felt the same way. All I wanted was to go out on my own. My father wanted me to follow in his footsteps, as I would like to see Albert do. Funny, some things don't change. What were the words I preached to him the other day? 'You need to make plans for your life.' It is possible he will go in another direction; he may start a new legacy of his own.*

He turned back to his son and grandson with a slight smile. "Albert, my boy, you take all the time you want. I'll back you in any way I can. Your father and I understand exactly how you feel and we want the best for you, whatever it is."

Albert was deeply affected by what his grandfather said. "I don't know yet what I will do, but I want you both to know whatever it turns out to be, I will always be grateful for your support. The last couple of days I have been thinking about America. Have you ever been there, Grandfather?"

"No, though I always wanted to. Now that I have the time, there is no longer the desire."

"The other day I met a man who said he was in the war there. He also said you and him used to play together when you were children."

"Bogie, ol' Bogie. Where did you find him? I haven't seen him in ages."

"He lives one mile or so from here. I was riding your fence line and before I knew it I was on his land. He said he was going to run me off his land but all he wanted was someone to talk to. I felt sorry for him. You know he lost his leg in the war."

"I know right where he lives and don't let him fool you about having only one leg. I wish I were half the man he is. There is no one I know that can out shoot him with either pistol or rifle. He is also the best with sword, cutlass, or any kind of weapon. We used to roam these hills for miles around. A better man you will never find, if he likes you."

"Hope you don't mind, sir, I studied your map of America and read the news clippings you have. Also, would you go with me to talk with Mr. Burton again?"

"I would surely like to visit with Bogie. Maybe tomorrow all three of us can go see my old friend."

Time for Albert seemed to stand still that afternoon. While his father and grandfather studied and talked about the family holdings, he decided to go to the stables to see Dap and maybe go for a ride. John, the man in charge of the stables, was in the process of shoeing Dap.

"You cannot trust these young boys to do this right, sir. They can do most things around here but not shoe a horse right, and this is most important in tending to a horse."

"John, have you ever been to America?"

"No, sir, nor do I want to. My father was killed there fighting in that terrible war. Never saw any sense in going to such a Godforsaken place."

When John finished with Dap, Albert thought it too late to

go for a ride. He led him back to his stable and gave him a complete rubdown. *If perchance I go away, what will Dap do? It will be hard to go and leave him. Maybe Father will want to ride and care for him.*

After spending an hour tending to his horse, he strolled back to the castle still thinking about that faraway country, America.

Albert was up early and went directly to the kitchen. Alma, the cook's help, was in the process of firing the large stove. She smiled and stated this time he did not surprised her. "I want to thank you, sir for giving me this job. It is so much better than working at the other place. Here I get to do a lot of the cooking, not just the cleaning. Can I fix you something to eat?"

"Not this morning. I will wait until Father and Grandfather are ready to eat."

"Lord Anderson is very punctual. He wants his morning meal at exactly eight o'clock."

Alma cooked the food and Albert followed her out to the smaller dining hall at precisely eight o'clock. His father and grandfather were entering the room as Alma rolled the cart next to the table. Albert was amazed at the precision with which this was carried out.

"Ready to go visit our neighbor?" Lord Anderson asked when he finished his last cup of tea.

"How do you get to Mr. Burton's house, Grandfather? I must have taken the long way before."

"There used to be a trail to his place if it's not overgrown," he answered.

When they mounted their horses, Lord Anderson took the lead. He soon found the path he was looking for. It was still good enough to travel, though in places they needed to make detours around overgrowth. A short distance from Bogie's cabin, Lord Anderson's horse stopped suddenly and reared almost dislodging him.

"What are you doing on my property without being invited?" someone yelled.

Lord Anderson quickly had his horse under control as Bogie stepped from behind a large oak.

"Al, is that you? I recognize the boy so it must be."

"Yes, Bogie, it is I, my son, Phillip, and grandson, Albert. We come to visit."

"You come to try and run me off my property. I know you Andersons."

"No, we didn't, Mr. Burton," Albert answered. "Just to visit. I want to talk to you more about America."

This appeased the old man. "Why didn't you say so? Get off them plugs and let's talk. Al, I haven't seen you in forever. You living back here now?"

Lord Anderson informed him he had been back in the castle four years.

"And you say this is your boy, Phillip?"

"Yes, Bogie, this is my son, Phillip. How have you been getting along?"

"You know me, Al, never a sick day in my life. What's this talk about America? You plan on going there?"

"Albert wants to talk to you about America, and no I don't plan on going there."

Bogie invited them to his house to talk seeing they were not there to run him off his property. They were asked to sit at the table while he made tea for them.

"What do you want to know, Sonny? Like I said the other day, I would be there now if I were not crippled. Never was a place like America. Of course, I never did see all of it, but what part I saw was splendid. Only thing, the people there have a mind of their own. All the land you want for nothing if you're not afraid of the Indians."

"Tell me about the Rocky Mountains. Did you actually see them?" Albert asked getting excited.

"Never saw the Rockies, though I did see the Smokies in the east. I talked to some trappers who lived out west. You should have seen them, real men. They trapped beaver and lived off the land. They came down in the summer, sold their hides, and went back to trap more each winter. You thinking of going to America, Sonny?"

Albert looked first at his father, then his grandfather to see if they would have an answer. He wanted more than anything to say yes, though he could not make the decision. "I don't know," is what he settled for.

"Can you shoot a gun? Could you kill to protect yourself if need be? You able to walk twenty miles a day with a heavy pack on your back? If not, you better stay here."

Albert did not know what to say. *Disillusioned for sure, yet he knew one day he would see America. Never had he shot a weapon of any kind and why would he ever have to kill a person? Bogie must be trying to scare me.*

The subject of America was dropped and Albert said no more. The visit continued for a while longer with Bogie asking most of the questions. "Al, you ever tell this boy our family secret?"

"No, and I am not going to. Let it die with us."

When the three took their leave, Bogie called out, "I'll teach you to shoot, the rest is up to you."

The three men stopped and turned their horses to face Bogie. "The rest is up to you," he repeated. That one statement filled Albert with all the anxiety he had before, and more. Now for sure he knew he would see America.

Both his father and grandfather were watching Albert. They knew at that moment Albert would be leaving them.

"I have to go," he said. "If Bogie will teach me, I will learn. Will you both give me your blessings?"

"This is all too fast," Lord Anderson, answered, "but if you are sure this is what you want, I wish you the best." His father also was in agreement.

"I shall see you this afternoon, Bogie," he called back.

Each of them were in deep thought on the ride back to the castle wondering what adventures were in store for Albert.

"I will make arrangements for the passage if you want, Son. Your grandfather knows what you will need for your training."

Lord Anderson did not like the fact Albert would be going so far away. *One thing I do like is that Bogie will know what is best for him. A week ago, I said he should grow up, now he is trying to do just that. I should be more careful of what I say.*

"Come with me, Albert," his grandfather said when they entered the castle. He went directly to his bedroom and closed the door. "I have a few important items you will need in training." A hidden room was revealed when a wardrobe was rolled aside. Albert could not believe all the things he saw.

"Where did all this come from, Grandfather?" He exclaimed. One wall was completely filled with firearms of all types, another with swords and knives, military uniforms, and things he did not even recognize.

"Some were given to me, others were purchased. My hobby over the years was collecting firearms. Your grandmother didn't like them around so I built this hidden room. For now, you can use a pistol and a good musket. When you are ready to leave, I will outfit you with other things."

Albert was beside himself. So happy one minute then fear tugged at him the next. *Am I leaving Father and Grandfather in a lurch when they need me?* He asked himself. *No, I have to go. It is my destiny. If I stay I will never be of use to myself or anyone else.*

After a hardy lunch, both Lord Anderson and Phillip watched as Albert left, riding Dap, a pistol in his belt and holding a musket.

"There he goes, Son, for better or worse. May God go with him."

CHAPTER FOUR

For a solid month, Albert felt like dead meat. The first week he thought he was going to die. Weekends he stayed at the castle. During the week, wherever night caught them was where they slept. Most of the time it would be in the woods, places where Albert had never been. He ran until he thought his legs would fall off. Bogie right beside or ahead of him all the way. He used a wooden leg he himself made. *Where did this man get his stamina?*

"When do we practice shooting?" Albert asked one evening. There was a light rain and both were soaked to the skin.

"Ready for that, are you? Where are we? How do we get home from here?" Bogie changed the subject.

"Don't you know?" Albert replied.

"I'm not sure. You take the lead and I will follow."

The first few days of training, Albert did not know where they were most of the time. Lately, he began to pay more attention when they entered a new area. He understood now he was being challenged. "I can't tell you exactly where we are, but if you can keep up, I will show you the way home." Without further discussion, Albert took off at a fast trot. Bogie kept pace for a ways then began to fall back. This excited Albert that distance was gained on Bogie. Four miles into the run, Albert could not hear anyone behind him. He stopped for Bogie to catch up. After a few minutes, nothing. No sound except for the rain. It was getting dark and Albert did not know what to do. They were still two miles from the cabin. Bogie always stressed if they were separated to go back to the cabin and wait. This is what he decided to do. When the cabin came in sight, there were lights showing in the windows. "How did you get ahead of me?" Albert asked entering the house. "Took the shortcut, Sonny, two kilometers shorter to be exact. Here, have some fresh tea and muffins from this morning. Tomorrow is Sunday, go home and be back Monday bright and early and we will learn how to use our firearms.

Albert was plenty tired when he arrived at the castle. Bogie did not allow him to ride Dap. "Run wherever you go," he had said. He dried himself with a towel, fell in bed and was asleep.

Albert was five minutes late for breakfast the next morning. His father and grandfather were already eating.

"Sorry, I had a hard time getting out of bed this morning."

"How is the training going, Son?" Phillip asked.

Albert filled them in on the things they were doing. "I don't understand how a seventy-year-old man with a wooden leg can do what Bogie does. He can outrun me, disappear any time right before my eyes, and never gets tired."

Lord Anderson laughed at what Albert said. "That was how it was when we were young. No way I could keep up with him. In the woods, he could outrun a man on a horse and hide where there was no place to hide. Stick with him, Son, and he will teach you these things."

"I can already see an improvement in myself, and if I live through this, maybe I'll survive America."

"When do you think you will want to leave for there?" Phillip asked.

"He hasn't said. I'll ask him. We are supposed to start shooting tomorrow."

Before dawn, Albert stepped onto Bogie's porch. He was sitting in the rocking chair sipping his tea. "How about something to eat, Sonny, before we get out the guns?"

"No thanks, I have already eaten. Bogie, when will we be ready to go to America? My father wants to know so he can book passage."

"We? I didn't say I was going. I agreed to train and teach you. As soon as you learn to shoot good enough, maybe another week."

"I thought you wanted to go with me. Grandfather thinks so too. Things won't be the same without you."

"I'm getting too old to be traipsing around in another world. It is nothing like anything you have ever seen. The country is wild and so are the people. There are grizzly bears the size of a coach, mountain lions can kill a horse and pack it off. Indians that will cut your scalp off while you are still alive."

Albert was devastated. He could see all of these things in his mind. *Surely the cities were civilized, and the settlers had to be normal people. I cannot change my plans now. If Bogie will not go, I will go alone.*

Bogie went inside to refill his cup. *I never told Albert I was going with him. Where would he get such a notion? What if he gets himself killed over there? I would be responsible and his grandfather would never forgive me. What have I to lose? There is nothing for me here. Just as well go and watch out for this youngster. He is a lot like Al, no quitting in him. He will go far in the new country.*

Albert was sitting on the steps in deep thought. "Changed my mind, Sonny. Go get your shooting gear. We have to get you ready for that wild country and in a hurry. You can tell your father to make his arrangements for passage anytime he wants. We'll be ready."

Albert could not believe his ears. He jumped and hugged Bogie before he realized what he was doing and yelled, "Thanks Bogie, thanks! What a time we will have, you and me mountain men. I will learn to shoot and shoot straight, I promise."

And he did. For two weeks from daylight till dark, Albert shot both rifle and pistol. He was not as accurate as Bogie, but almost.

One more thing he had to do before he left was to go see his mother. Albert's mother was glad to see him. He had not visited her since Miss Margaret moved into the same house. "I have been quite busy lately, Mother. Do you know Mr. Burton? We are going to America. He has been teaching me to shoot and how to survive in the wild. We are leaving as soon as arrangements can be made and I wanted to see you before we left. How are you doing?"

"Things are fine. Margaret and I have learned a hard lesson and we talk about it often. We now realize how like little girls we were. I want to apologize for the way we acted and would like to do the same to Lord Anderson and Phillip as well, though I am embarrassed to go to them. Could you tell them for me I'm sorry?"

"Yes, Mother, I will do it. Is there anything I can do for you before I leave for America?"

"Just keep me informed as to what you are doing, and Son, I love you. I have never said that to anyone before. I hope it is not too late." Albert wrapped his arms around his mother and said, "I love you too, Mother."

After a couple hours of conversation, Albert could tell she

had really changed.

"Dap," he said on the way back to the castle. "Looks like things are working out fine. The only thing that would make this perfect is to have you go with me"

Albert decided to go to the Knob one more time. He pointed Dap towards the hill and let him run. The sun was warm and the scenery beautiful. Albert dismounted when they reached the top to let Dap catch his breath. He wondered if America looked anything like this. The castle loomed huge in the distance. *I'll bet there isn't anything like this where I'm going.* Dap was in rare form loping down to the stable. He headed straight towards the stone fence and leaped over as he did so often. "What a horse. I will ask Grandfather if he will ride you while I am away."

After personally caring for Dap, Albert went to the castle. There sitting with his grandfather was Bogie. "I was hoping you would get here soon. We sent for Bogie. Your ship sails tomorrow afternoon. Bogie is packed and ready. The only thing left is you and your horses, if you want to take them."

Albert could not believe his luck and he showed his excitement. "I thought taking Dap too much to ask for. I will hurry and get my things."

Wait just a moment, Son. The guns you practiced with are not the ones you will be taking. I have much better ones to give you. Bogie picked out what you will need for getting along in America."

This was the third time today exceptionally good things happened. Then he thought of what his mother asked of him. "Grandfather, Mother wanted me to tell you she is sorry for the way she acted in the past and if you would forgive her. I feel she really means it."

"We will see," is all he would say.

The next morning Bogie picked the horse he wanted and the horses and their possessions were loaded on the cargo ship. The captain made it plain the animals were their responsibility. "There is enough hay and grain for the voyage," the captain stated.

With their goodbyes said, the two men climbed the catwalk to the upper deck watching as the mooring lines were cast off. Parts of the sails were hoisted and the ship began to move away from the landing. "Can't back out now, Sonny. Hope this is what you want."

"Grandfather told me I needed to figure out what I wanted to do with my life and I think this is it. At least I am going to give it a try. Bogie, thanks for coming with me."

"Let's go talk to the captain, Sonny. He wants all passengers to meet in the dining area soon after we get underway."

There were six men passengers and a black man who was introduced only as Ben. Captain Watts believed women on board would cause a plague.

"I believe you all know my rules. You tend to your own stock. If you have firearms that are not in my possession, give them over to Ben. This is a must. This room and the upper deck are available for you to lounge in. There will be no liquor or gambling allowed. This is a cargo ship, though we do take on passengers at times. If you need anything or have questions, see Ben. That will be all."

"Boy, he is a cranky old man," someone said.

"He's been sailing over forty years, and he knows what he's doing," Ben answered. "If I can help in any way, come talk to me."

Bogie asked if he could find something for him and Albert

to do, it would make the time go faster.

"Not many people want to work," Ben answered smiling, showing his perfect white teeth. "I'll see about that." He motioned them to follow him. On the deck, he looked around to make sure no one could hear. "Most of our sailors are good men, but not all. Keep a sharp eye and keep your door locked." Albert thanked him for the warning.

"We better listen to him, Sonny. Keep your money on you at all times, and like I taught you, be aware of those around you."

Ben asked if they would like to help secure the cargo in the ships hold. It is next to where the livestock are held. "Meet me there in ten minutes and I can show you what to do."

Dap knew Albert's voice instantly when he called out to him. "I know you don't like being on this ship. Neither do I. It won't last forever." The horses were tended while Ben waited to show them what was needed in the hold.

"Usually the cargo is hurriedly moved in here. After we get under way, we organize and secure it with ropes. If we don't, the first storm will damage the whole lot." He showed how the crates were to be placed and secured to the hooks with rope. The first day passed fast. When Albert and Bogie entered their room, they knew instantly someone had gone through their luggage. Whoever it was tried to place things back in order.

"I am glad you told me to keep my money with me, Bogie, or it would all be gone now. That was a good idea. You think we should report this break in?"

"Not now, Sonny. I am for trying to catch whoever it is. Hide your money in this room. He has already looked here. This can be dangerous if he thinks we are carrying it on us. Don't act suspicious but stay on your toes."

Nothing happened the next two days. Each evening, after eating, they would go to the upper deck for a while. The third day turned out to be different. As usual, they ate and went on the deck. The moment they closed the door, two men jumped them. A much larger man quickly knocked Bogie to the floor. Albert was stunned by a blow to the head but managed to stay on his feet. "Help me with this kid, Pete. The old cripple can't do anything." Pete kicked Bogie in the ribs and moved to help his partner. That was a mistake. Bogie removed his wooden leg and hopped into them swinging it like a club. The first blow knocked Pete over the ship's rail. Albert was pounding on the other man, one of the passengers. The commotion alerted the attention of the others. First on the scene was Ben. He was ready for action and disappointed it was over.

Ben brought them to the captain's office to explain the incident. "Pete is no great loss," The captain said. "Leave this one with me. He will take Pete's place until I can turn him over to the authorities. Ben knows how to handle his kind."

The rest of the voyage was without incident. The weather treated them good and in six weeks they saw the shoreline of Newfoundland. With the voyage ahead of schedule and having a good tail wind, the captain decided not to stop for supplies. Three days later, Nova Scotia was sighted. In five days more, they reached the destination, Portsmouth on the coast of Virginia, to deliver their cargo. The half dozen passengers with their belongings were allowed to leave the ship first.

"Do you feel dizzy like you're about to fall over?" Albert asked when they were off the ship.

"It won't take long to get your land legs back, Sonny. The first thing we have to do is find a strong pack horse to carry our goods. Until we do, let's load my horse. I am sure glad I talked

Al out of bringing all the stuff he thought was needed."

They were able to get the majority on Bogie's horse. The last bundle, they fastened on Dap who was not the least bit happy.

"The prices here in town are too high to buy what we need. Let's go out a ways to the farms and do business with them."

After they left the docking area, there were people from street urchins to the high society, walking and riding. There were wagons and buggies of all descriptions filling the streets.

"Look over there, Bogie," Albert said pointing to a small group of men. "Are those mountain men? They're dressed like you described and all of them have long rifles."

"Could be, though not the kind we are looking for. This is too far east."

After going through the main part of town, there were less people and businesses. Farms with all sorts of animals began to appear more often. Towards evening, they crossed a bridge and a fast-flowing stream. A lane led to a house and large barn that could be seen from the main road. Bogie said he was getting tired and wanted to see if they could possibly stay the night and buy what they needed to go on. Two growling dogs met them at the gate. Bogie, paying no attention, tied the horses to a rail, opened the gate and walked in with Albert nervously following. An elderly couple sitting on their porch said nothing till they reached the steps.

"Kind of nervy walking in on them dogs, ain't you boys?"

"Those dogs are not bad," Bogie answered. "They are just doing their job. What would be the chance of sleeping in your barn tonight and buying a few supplies?"

"The dogs let you in so I guess it's okay. What kind of things you want to buy?"

"Where are your manners, George? Can't you see one of them is crippled?"

You most certainly can sleep in our barn, though no fire. If you want to eat, we have leftovers."

"We thank you kindly, ma'am, and yes, we haven't eaten since morning."

Greta placed the food and tea on the table. While answering questions, Albert and Bogie ate their fill of the best food since they left England.

"What a fine couple these people are," Albert stated, "to take in strangers, feed and give them a place to sleep. I believe I am going to like America."

Though Bogie did not say anything, his instincts told him George and Greta were not the people Albert thought they were. He tried to get Albert's attention but he was too busy talking. Bogie suspected Greta was up to something and poured his tea into the cat's bowl when Greta was not watching. "Look at him now, sleeping like a baby."

After eating, they went to feed and care for their horses and then to the tack room to turn in. Bogie soon realized their situation. He checked the door lock; it could only be opened from the outside. There were no windows. *I must find a way to get out of here, and fast.* One wall inside the barn was wide oak boards that possibly could be pried loose. He quickly searched the barn for something which could be forced between the boards, the only thing was a short-handled spade. A light got his attention and then he heard voices. Quickly Bogie grabbed the spade, closed the door, and jumped in bed with the spade, hoping it would work.

"Sound asleep," George said, laughing. "You sure know how to pick the good ones. The old one-legged gent ain't much but the young fellow will bring a pretty penny."

"Make sure the door is locked. We'll send for old Briggs tomorrow and see what he offers for them and the horses."

It was getting dark in the little room. Bogie tried pushing the spade between the cracks; the boards were too close together. Trying other boards, he found one with the crack almost wide enough. There was nothing in the room to pound with.

My leg sure is a handy tool. Lightly he hammered the spade between the boards. The board did not move, the spade bent. *That didn't work. I'll try something else. Why didn't I think to use the spade the way it is meant to be used?*

For two hours, Bogie searched the little room and tried different things, though nothing worked. By three o'clock in the morning he had almost given up. He thought about the lock. The way it was made, one little iron pin held the latch in place. *Did George forget to place the pin in the hole?*

He found a small piece of the spade that was broken off. The latch was visible. Slipping it under the metal under the bar, he gently lifted. It moved. George had forgotten to pin the lock. He gently opened the door. "Albert, wake up." Rising and shaking, Albert moaned. "Time to get up, Sonny. We got a lot to do."

"What is going on, Bogie? It is still dark outside and I feel terrible."

"Get up and move around. You will feel better."

Albert wobbled across the room and sat on the bed again. "Get yourself up, Sonny, we have a lot of work to do."

He managed to get up and follow Bogie out the door where they found a lamp. Now, you saddle the horses while I find a pack-horse. He picked a strong looking roan and a pack-saddle. Soon all their supplies were in place and they were ready to go.

Albert began to collect his senses and wanted to know what they were doing.

"Tell you about it later. We will wait behind this hay for our friends." At daylight, Greta and George came to check on them. George had a pistol. She unlocked the door and saw the prisoners were gone.

"Surprise, surprise," Bogie exclaimed, wrenching the pistol from George. "I thought you would be here earlier." They could not understand what was going on.

"We have a little business to address then we will be leaving. Shall we go to the house where it is more comfortable?"

After they entered the house, Bogie had them sit. "There is a blue roan horse out there with a pack saddle that is worth maybe sixty pounds."

"Sixty pounds of what?" George asked.

"Oh, I forgot. You have dollars instead of real money. If I remember right, it would be a little more. We will call it eighty dollars. Write out a bill of sale and we will call things even."

"That's not right," George said getting all excited. "I won't do it."

"Then tell me where the nearest law is and we will go and talk to them."

"George, we have been out smarted. We can't win them all." Greta said with a cackle. "Write the bill of sale."

Hesitantly, he did what he was told.

"Where you boys going?" Greta asked.

"West, to the Rockies," Albert related, finally feeling like himself.

"You mind if I get a few things together and come along? I kind of like you men."

"You can't up and leave me, Greta. What will I do without you?"

"I was just funning, George, just funning."

Bogie and Albert headed towards the Rockies with their supplies, a good pack-horse and bill of sale.

CHAPTER FIVE

Outdoor life agreed with the two men. They rode mostly but Bogie insisted they keep up their physical training, so two hours running was the order of each day. Most people wore leather shoes called moccasins made by the Indians that were readily available, very cheap and easy to run in.

The days turned into weeks, they traveled into what the people called the Smoking Mountains. Many friendly and helpful Cherokee Indian tribes lived throughout the area. "These are the biggest mountains I have ever seen," Albert stated the second day. "If the Rockies are larger, how can a person find their way?"

"There must be ways, Sonny. We will have to learn them if we are to be mountain men."

On and on they went week after grueling week, always west.

They learned to live off the land. With the help of people they met, they learned to cure their meat, make their own clothing and live with nature. They stopped where the people invited them in, white and Indian alike. Some had no time for them and asked them to move on. They did. Albert learned to shoot with accuracy and wild meat became his responsibility to provide. His mind became as keen as the animals he hunted and his body developed into a man, strong and muscular. Many of the days he never mounted Dap. Pacing himself at a trot, he could go for hours, mile after mile. "How much further can this plain go with nothing but grass, Bogie? You said this country was large but that is an understatement. Do you think people will ever settle all this land?"

"One day there will be people out here. Maybe not in our lifetime, but one day."

A few nights later their horses woke them. Something was all around snorting and making loud grunts. A herd of buffalo had surrounded them while they were asleep. "What shall we do, Bogie?"

"Keep the horses quiet and wait. So far, they are the only ones excited."

The sun came up and the buffalo still came. The horses had gotten use to them. The dust became so thick they had to wet towels for them and the horses to breathe through. Late afternoon the last ones passed.

"The people in England would never believe this, Sonny. Unless I seen it, I don't think I would."

A few days later they saw what looked like huge mountains in the far distance. "I bet that's the Rockies, Bogie. Can you make them out?"

"I kind of see something. Give it a few more days."

On clear days, the mountains were plain to see with the snow caps. The west winds were cold and the men had no heavy coats. The grassy plains turned to sage and rocky outcropping and the two determined men kept going. The closer to the mountains they got, the larger they became. Bogie and Albert were in the foothills when they saw them; Indians on horses, just watching.

"Pay them no mind, Sonny. Make like you don't see them."

It was scary and hard to do. When they approached the Indians, they let them pass.

"It's your leg, Bogie. They are looking at your wooden leg."

"If they are interested, let's show them how it works."

They stopped and Bogie unstrapped his leg and held it up. The Indians began to point and laugh. One of them dismounted and reached out to touch it. He carefully examined the leg and handed it back. He said something neither Albert nor Bogie understood and then motioned for them to follow. Two miles further and they were at their village. Indians of all sizes surrounded them. The ones they followed dismounted. Bogie and Albert did likewise. In front of the largest teepee, a lone man stood with his arms crossed. The Indians addressed him and he looked at Bogie and made a guttural sound. Bogie thought that he also wanted to look at his leg so he took it off. There was a lot of discussion among the Indians. He handed it to the lone Indian, who also examined it. He then motioned them into his teepee. He sat, and then Bogie and Albert sat. That was when they got a surprise.

"You make this?" he asked.

"Yes, I made it."

"Can you make one for him?" He pointed at a little boy sitting on a bed of animal skins.

"Can the boy speak English?"

"I can speak your language, and mine. My name means Hunting Boy in your language, though later when I am bigger, I will get my real name. You can call me Boy for now. This is my father. He is our Chief."

Bogie in turn gave his and Albert's name and asked Boy if he would come and show him his leg. It had been taken off below the knee by an army doctor to save the boy's life. He used a crutch to get around.

"Can you run?" the boy asked getting excited.

"Come outside and I'll show you."

"Who can run the fastest here?" Bogie asked.

"Him," Boy pointed at a tall young man.

Ask him if he wants to run with me. To the biggest tree and back." Boy said something and the young man smiled and came over.

"We call him Runner because he can run faster than anyone. He says you are a cripple and does not want you to be laughed at."

"Tell him this is just for fun and to show the people what a cripple person can do."

All was explained and when Boy said "go" the race would start.

Bogie and his competition stood side-by-side and waited. There was absolute quiet.

"Go."

Both started at the same time. Bogie increased his pace and the other matched him. Neither one wanted to show out. Bogie went faster, then faster. The other runner stayed by his side. They rounded the tree and Bogie went all out, he had not been challenged like this in a long time. They reached the finish together, both breathing hard. The village went crazy with yelling and patting both runners on the back. When things settled down, Albert, Bogie, Boy and his father went back to their teepee.

"Can you help me run like that?" Boy asked again excitedly. Bogie told him he would make him a wooden leg and the rest would be up to him.

"You make me a leg and I will learn to run like you."

"We will look for the right kind of wood tomorrow and you can help."

Albert and Bogie were asked to stay with the Chief, whose name was White Wolf. He was named White Wolf because his father was a white man who married into the Ute tribe. He taught all who wanted to learn the white man's language and there were still several of the older ones who could speak and understand it.

White Wolf's wife died from an avalanche the past winter in the same accident where Boy hurt his leg. His foot was mangled and infection set in. The Army doctor at the fort said the boy's life could possibly be saved though he would have to remove the foot and part of his leg.

What a bad turn for the little tyke, Bogie thought. *I will do my best to help him run, and if I am any judge of people, he will do his best also.*

Their supplies were brought into their teepee and the horses turned loose with the Indians' horses.

"You talk strange talk. You talk English but not very good." White Wolf commented. "Where are you from?"

"Have you ever heard of England? That is where Bogie and I come from."

They had not heard of it and wanted to know where it was and how far away.

Bogie held up both hands closing and opening them five times. "This many days on a ship across the ocean." He drew on the ground the two continents with water between. "Many, many more days walking and riding to get here."

"Why do you go to so much trouble to come here? What are you looking for?"

"We come to see your big mountains and to trap beaver,"

Albert answered. "Do you know any mountain men? People who live in the high mountains?"

White Wolf began to understand and thought, *This boy don't know what's in store for him, though this Bogie is old enough to know.* He grunted and smiled. "Not many people can live a winter in the high mountains. They mostly die and never come down. The beaver are not plentiful like they once were, almost gone."

The talk went on, each asking and answering questions.

That night it snowed, the biggest snowstorm of the season. The next morning a hunt for buffalo was planned. Albert wanted to know if he could be a part of the hunt. "You can go," the Chief answered, "If you want to live here, you need to learn the ways of our people."

Albert was excited when they asked him to go with them. The day before, a scouting party from their village had located a herd not far away. Unless they were frightened, they would probably still be in the vicinity. Each hunter rode his favorite horse on the hunt. They brought Dap up to the Chief's teepee for Albert. None of the Indians used saddles and only one had a blanket. Albert had never ridden bare back before and decided to try it. The party of twelve hunters rode in the direction where the buffalo were last seen. A mile from their village, they came across a dozen cows with half grown calves and three large bulls. They were excited to see them this close and wondered if they could drive them closer. A runner went back to alert the village to what was going on. The hunters positioned themselves on three sides leaving the end open toward camp. The animals started to move. About half way, a cow turned and started running. The hunters, yelling with excitement, began to shoot their arrows and buffalo started falling. Albert was an excellent shot and Dap kept him within easy range of the ones too far to shoot with bow and arrow. In less than twenty minutes, they had most of what they needed for the winter and Albert had killed almost half. The village was in a jubilant spirit and the women were happy the meat was so close because they did most of the butchering.

"What are these kids doing?" Bogie asked the chief when the children brought limbs and chunks of wood to the middle of the village. "They will make a feast to celebrate a successful hunt." A large bonfire made it easy for all the people to roast their favorite choice of meat. The excitement lasted into the night. Everyone ate their fill and told their stories, contributing their luck to the two white men who befriended their village.

For the next week, the whole tribe worked with the killed buffalo. The hides were de-fleshed and stretched in the sun to dry. Strips of meat hung on green willow sticks and smoked. The leaner portions of the meat were made into pemmican, a delicacy that would last for months. Thin strips were dried and ground into a powder, mixed with rendered fat and dried berries. It was a high protein food.

Albert worked alongside the Indians trying to learn their ways and customs.

These people lived the same generation after generation; living off the land, wasting nothing and not asking for anything more.

Bogie and Boy were now inseparable. They found an aspen tree the size needed for a wooden leg. "It will hurt for a while, until your leg toughens where it's in contact with the wood. Give it two weeks and that part will be over. Then the real work will start. You are lucky you still have a bendable knee. If it were cut above the knee, things would be bad. This is going to take a while but I will help you."

"How long did it take for you to learn to walk and run?"

"About a year. I fought it and almost gave up. I won't let you do the same."

The only tool to work with was a knife Bogie had. The process was slow, though after a couple of days, it began to take shape. The leg was small compared to Bogie's and Boy thought this funny.

CHAPTER SIX

Albert captured the admiration of all the warriors and young men of the tribe. His strength of body and accuracy with his rifle won them over. The unmarried girls also vied for his attention, each trying to outdo the other. He soon received several new buffalo coats, all too small for his broad shoulders.

"It will take a complete hide to make him a coat," Runner, said. "Maybe two."

The first to make one fit was Singing Dove, the most beautiful of them all.

"Thank you," Albert stated when the coat fit his broad shoulders perfectly. She had removed the hair and bleached the softened hide till it was almost white. The front overlapped and leather strings tied it secure.

"You are in trouble now, my friend," someone exclaimed, and they all laughed.

Winter came with a vengeance. The snow which piled four and five feet against the north side of the teepees helped to keep them warm. Bogie finished carving the wooden leg for Boy. "If you want, keep the crutch until you learn to steady yourself. It will take a while to be able to balance and not fall."

He tried without the crutch and found it was better with it.

"Don't put too much weight on the leg. It will toughen in time and before long, you will be able to do most anything."

With the snow so deep outside, Boy walked around and around inside the teepee with a big smile. His father, White Wolf, was very pleased and thanked Bogie for making it possible for his son to walk and maybe to run again.

The snow did not keep the men from hunting. Large herds of elk came off the mountain and the hunters killed enough to fill their winter supply of meat.

Albert and Runner were becoming close friends. Each day, weather permitting, they would ride off together. Sometimes to hunt and other times just to look around. Albert learned a bit of the Ute language and Runner could speak and understand much of the English.

"Have you ever been up there? Albert asked one day, pointing toward the mountains.

"Yes, several times, though not in the winter. Them who do never come back. The spirits don't allow no one up there when it starts to snow."

"What about the men who live and trap beaver? The ones they call mountain men? They spend the winter up there."

"Maybe white men can, though my people cannot."

"Have you ever met them who live up there?"

"I have been to a cabin where it is said a white trapper once lived. It is high up where only in the summer can you get there. They say the snow completely covers it in the winter. Why do you want go to a place like that?"

"I know you don't understand I must try to do this. I myself don't know why. I only know it is something I have to do. Can you tell me exactly where this cabin is?"

"When do you want to go?"

"As soon as possible before it snows again. I will talk to my friend, Bogie, and White Wolf first. Then you can draw me a map to guide me."

Albert felt relieved knowing his long-awaited dreams were now going to be fulfilled, one way or another. Maybe the spirits would welcome him, if not, so be it.

It was midday when they arrived back at the village. Albert wasted little time telling Bogie what he had decided to do.

"Why don't you wait until winter is over, Sonny, then both of us will go as planned. I don't think I can handle this much snow."

"Don't think me ungrateful, Bogie. This is my dream. You got me this far and now it is up to me. I will remember what you taught me and will be forever in your debt. I do not plan to do any trapping, just spend the rest of the winter up there."

"There are many things that can kill you, my friend," Chief White Wolf exclaimed. "The grizzly bear kills many people. Most are now asleep in their den, though some are not. He doesn't see too well but he can hear and smell better than you and will come from behind. He will be the hunter. The mountain lion is also to be feared. They are hungry in the cold days of winter and will hunt anything, but the worst thing of all will be the cold, the snow and the isolation. No one to talk to, only yourself."

"Runner said there was a cabin up there."

"I know the cabin. It is a good one, though the spirits live there. I will tell you what I know. Almost twenty years ago, a white man came to our village. He was looking for gold. My sister fell in love with him and they were married. They went high up in the mountains to find what he was looking for. That was the last time I saw her. Three years went by and I climbed the mountain to find her. What I found was her grave. Her husband said she died in childbirth. There was a little girl, but I believe the spirits took her. Do what you want, but be careful. The spirits of the old ones are real and if they are calling, you must go."

Albert explained that Runner was going to draw a map to show how to get to the trapper's cabin high up the mountain. The rest of the day was spent gathering supplies and food. Runner and two other braves agreed to go with him as far as the horses could go, then it would be up to him.

That evening, Bogie asked Albert to come and sit. He had something to tell him. "It's the family secret I think you should know about and I believe your grandfather would approve. I am your great uncle. Al and I are half-brothers. I am really an Anderson. My mother was a servant at the castle, and when she told my father she was expecting a child, he quickly paid her a little money and told her to get out. She later married Beauregard Burton, my stepfather. He never claimed me, though he gave me his name and was always ready to let me and everyone else know I was not his child. My mother told me the truth about it and she spent the rest of her life a very unhappy woman. I hold no grudges, Albert, though my mother and I were wronged. I wish you and I could have gotten together years ago. I promised your father and grandfather I would take care of you on this journey and I don't like to see you going off by yourself, though I know this is what you came here for. Be careful and do not take any foolish chances. I will be here when you get back."

Next morning, the four men left the village on horseback leading a packhorse loaded with the supplies. They would go as far as the horses could go and then return home. That evening, they camped in the foothills of the mountain. The wind had swept the greater part of the snow into drifts which allowed them to go farther than expected. The next evening, they came to where the trail was too narrow for the horses. They spent the night trying to convince Albert to come back to the village and wait until spring to do this.

"I have come a long way for this." He told them of the ship voyage and the hundreds of miles on foot and horseback. They listened in awe as Albert related in detail these wild adventure tales. "You understand now I have this to do?" They agreed with him, though they did not understand why he could not wait until spring.

The next morning, the hard thing for Albert was to send Dap back with the others. He did not want to leave his master and tried to break loose. Runner did not want to leave either and offered to go on with him. "No, my friend, I will see you when the snow melts and the grass turns green again."

Some of the supplies were stashed to be brought up later. The rest were carried in a large pack over a hundred pounds of weight. The climb was steep and the trail narrow. The pack rubbing against rock on one side and a thousand foot drop on the other. "Am I being a stubborn fool?" he asked himself.

Albert was glad for his heavy coat Singing Dove had made and the high-top leather boots the other girls gave him.

The wind blew cold even though the sun was shining bright. It took him an hour to go two miles up the narrow trail where the mountainside gave way to a meadow filled with white aspens. "This is the first landmark on my map." The drawings Runner gave him were etched in his mind. About one foot of snow covered the ground with deeper drifts against the outcrops. "Through this meadow and turn right to where I can see the huge black boulder standing like a teepee."

When the boulder came into sight, so did the largest bear he had ever seen. The wind was in his favor and the bear never saw him. It slowly made its way in the opposite direction Albert was going.

"I have to remember what I was told about bears circling to get behind a person."

There was still a lot of wildlife in the area, which Albert was glad of. He needed at least one big elk or three deer to supplement his rations, not to mention all the firewood to last the winter. An hour before dark, he located an overhang which had been used by someone before. Its size was perfect and gathering wood took little time. "Must have come a third of the way. Two days like today should bring me close to the cabin." The fire made the area inside cozy. "A metal cup to melt snow to drink and a bit of pemmican is all I need for tonight. When I get to the cabin there will be time to cook a good meal." With extra wood to keep the fire going through the night, Albert wrapped himself in a blanket and was soon asleep.

The next morning, the sun, bright against the snow, made it hard to see. He remembered the Indians talking about snow blindness. They made a mask with two small holes to see through. This helped very little but was better than nothing. That night, a few large boulders were all he could find for a place to camp. It was not as good as the night before.

"I hope this will be the day." Then it hit him. "What if the cabin is not there? Maybe someone has already claimed it. What will I do?" Only a minute did he worry, it was not his nature. "I will cross that bridge when I get to it."

Early afternoon the trail disappeared into the side of a cliff. "I must have taken a wrong turn somewhere." A little further on he realized the path went around and through what looked to be the side of the mountain. "Boy, am I glad I didn't turn and go back." About fifty yards through a natural tunnel, he entered the most beautiful place he had ever seen. The cabin, nestled in a small cove on the south side of the rock wall he came through, seemed to be vacant. The north and west wind could not reach it. A barn, larger than the house, was without a doubt, built by the same person. Stone and thick logs were used in the construction of them both.

The valley continued for half a mile and rounded a bend. About half the slope up the mountain was covered with pine and aspens.

"Whoever built these buildings knew how to build. The house was small enough to heat, yet big enough to live in. "Wonder who lived here and why did they leave? Could the spirits have something to do with it?"

There was no lock on the door, just a latch that could be opened from either side. It was dark and freezing inside. An oil lamp sat on the table beside a box of matches. "Someone must have known I was coming. I have to admit this is a little spooky."

Albert lit the lamp and saw a note on the table. *Welcome friend. Use what you need, replace it when you leave and keep things clean and tidy.* It was signed "Jim Butcher." A fireplace, already stacked with wood, served as heat and stove. The dry wood caught fire easily and Albert filled a kettle with snow and hung it over the fire. "I'll check this place out while the water heats." Two single beds on opposite ends of the room had curtains, which could be pulled to encircle the beds. There were no windows, just a front and back door. He opened the back door, entering a cave that could not be seen from outside. Firewood was stacked shoulder high as far as he could see. "I can say this, Mr. Butcher believed in being prepared. There is enough wood to last three years. When I get settled, I will check this cave out some more."

The hot water warmed his insides and the fire was warming the room. "If only Jim Butcher were a tea drinker, all would be perfect. I don't see how these Americans drink bitter coffee. I guess I still miss the good things of England."

Albert was getting hungry from not eating a whole meal for the last three days. "First, before it gets dark, I should have a look around outside." For the last few months, he had learned one never went anywhere without a rifle, anything could happen anytime. The barn intrigued him so he started there. Everything needed for a small ranch or farm was there. "This gets more interesting all the time. Why would anyone up and leave all this? Maybe I will figure it out before I go back down come spring." He started back to the cabin and saw several deer with their heads up watching him. "No better time than now to get the meat for the days to come. If the snow gets as deep as they say, the animals will leave here."

He shot a young buck. The others ran a short distance and stopped. "I will field dress and hang him in the barn for tonight. In the morning, I can start curing the meat." Albert learned from the Indians the heart, liver, and tongue were the tastiest parts. He would cook this for his supper.

The tongue and heart he boiled in salty water until tender for the next day. The liver was broiled over the hot coals and was quickly consumed. There was ground coffee that he boiled in a pot. "Maybe if I added sugar it would be drinkable." It was better, though not as good as tea.

The cabin warmed up considerably and for the first time in several nights he slept warmly.

The deer was gone the next morning. Something had

chewed through the leather straps and dragged it away. "I am sure I latched the door. Whoever or whatever it was had to unlatch it, break the ties and be strong enough to carry it away." When Albert went outside, he saw no sign.

"He must have come in the back." Sure enough, a trail in the snow revealed a mountain lion was the culprit. The lion had stopped a few yards from the barn and eaten a large portion of the deer. "This is a huge fellow judging by the tracks. There is not enough room here for us both and I don't plan on leaving." He followed the tracks for a while but decided this was not the smart thing to do. "The old boy will be back for a free meal when he's hungry and I will be ready for him." The remaining part was hung back in the barn.

The snow began to fall and the wind picked up before Albert got back to the cabin. With nothing more he could do outside, he decided to explore the cave. Where the wood was stacked, the cave was at least fifteen feet wide. There was more firewood than he first thought. "It must have taken him two years to cut and haul all of this wood." A smaller tunnel branched off to the right. "This was made by someone. There are pick marks." The ceiling was only four or five feet and he could see the end of the tunnel. "That will be a job for later." The main cave began to get smaller as it went on. Then he saw light from the outside, just a little. Large rocks were placed at the end and some had fallen away. Albert moved a few more and looked out. A shear drop of forty feet with a wide valley beyond is what he saw. "This has to be where the meadow turned where I entered. There must be a hundred acres here and I don't even know about the other direction. Mr. Butcher has himself a showplace here, but where is he?" The rocks were replaced so that no light showed and Albert returned to the cabin. He made himself another bit of American coffee, pulled a chair by the fire and drank. "Not like English tea, but it will do."

It was snowing harder so he placed another piece of wood on the fire and began to reason. *Why am I here at this particular place?* Watching the blaze and sparks from the fire put him in a trance. He saw himself as another person in another world. *The questions Grandfather asked me which I could not answer. What were my goals, my plans for the future, my ambitions? What was I going to make of myself? He was right; these things had never entered my mind. Where would I be now if he had not talked to me? I hate to think of that now, and what about Father? Would he still be at the hospital? What of Grandfather and Mother? So much has happened since those questions. It seems like years since then.* Another piece on the fire, more thinking, more wood. *Why did I come to America? I could have stayed in Europe just as well. Is there a purpose for me here in these mountains? More questions I cannot answer.*

The fire was almost out when he realized it was getting dark. He built it up again and thought of the lion. The rifle and single shot pistol were checked. Albert, carrying his rifle, made his way to the barn without making a sound. The Indians had taught him how. He entered the barn and holding the rifle ready in his right hand, cautiously reached behind to latch the door. *No need to give him two ways to get in.* Never had Albert heard a scream like that before. Instantly he froze; every muscle tense, only the eyes moving. Slowly he sat the lamp down. A blur caught his eye and he reacted instantly, a loud noise, then pain. The cold and pain awakened him. The lamp was still making a light or was it the sun? *Where am I? And why does my head hurt so badly?* Then he remembered the lion. *Where was the lion?* He tried to move his legs and could not. There across his legs was the lion, blood dried on its mouth and one eye shot out. It took a while to get his legs loose and make his way back to the cabin. Only a few coals were in the fireplace and it seemed to take forever to build up the fire. The warm wet cloth on his face lessened the pain across his forehead. He had seen a mirror by the other bed hanging from a nail. The room was dark so he went outside with the mirror where the sun was shining. Albert could not believe the person he saw was himself. *What a mess.* His thick black hair matted with blood; two, or was it three deep claw marks clotted over across his forehead. A large lump on the back of his head hurt the worst. His hair and beard were longer than he thought. *What an awful sight you are, Albert Anderson.*

His Ute Indian friends had given him a pouch of herbs in case he hurt himself. "Thank the Lord. Now where did that come from? I very seldom thank him for anything, though it may be time I started."

His cleanup took a while. When the room was warm again, he stripped and bathed as best he could without a tub, put on his only change of clothes, and went to the spring and washed his dirty things. "You know something, Albert, I think you may live a little longer if you leave those lions alone." The Utes talked about how good lion meat was and the claws and teeth were used in making necklaces. "The old boy ate my deer and turnabout is fair play."

The lion was at least nine feet long from the head to the tip of his tail and weighed almost two hundred pounds. While Albert was skinning the lion, he thought of how close he came to dying last night. *Did I get lucky? Maybe the spirits are protecting me. If so, why? Then he remembered the intense training with Bogie and realized what he owed to the lightening reflexes that had saved him.* He shoved the hay into the top of the barn back enough to stretch the hide on the floor. "This will make a fine shirt or something if I can tan it right." The huge claws came off easily but the teeth were a problem. A hammer and a chisel were a great help to remove the four fangs, one of which was half missing. He cut the meat into strips and hung it in front of the fireplace to dry. The day ended as Albert was finishing with the meat. He cleaned the claw wounds on his forehead and smeared it with a salve he found in the tack room in the barn. *Probably for animals*, he thought.

In the middle of the night, horse whinnying awakened him. In a flash, Albert was half dressed with a pistol in his hand. "Mr. Butcher must be back. I sure hope he is friendly." The horse sounded again, and closer this time. "I know that horse, but it can't be." He quickly opened the door, and sure enough, there stood Dap shaking his head up and down just like he used to do when he was around Albert. "How in the world did you ever find me? Did you come up the narrow trail? Never mind. You're here and that's what counts. You crazy, wonderful, old friend. Let's go to the barn and get you settled. A good rubdown and a generous amount of hay is all I can do for you tonight. In the morning, I will look you over and see if there are any problems."

The first thing Albert thought the next morning was, *What if there is another lion around? That's all we need.* Cautiously, he approached the barn with his rifle at the ready. Dap was anxiously waiting. There were no visible signs of injuries. Oats were found in a wooden barrel. Dap enjoyed them while he received another rubdown. "You have to fend for yourself as much as possible. There is a lot of good grass under the snow and you will have to paw it out." Albert knew Dap would not run away so he turned him loose. He had grazed with the Indians horses and knew how to find the grass.

Albert returned to the cabin and cleaned the wound where the lion had clawed him. It turned red during the night and looked infected when he saw it in the mirror. He boiled the herbs the Utes gave him, soaked a cloth with it and held it against the wound. *I can't let this get out of hand. If only Bogie were here, he would know what to do. Uncle Bogie. One never knows what secrets are hidden in a person's family. There is no doubt he's telling the truth about being an Anderson.*

That afternoon Albert began to run a fever and felt terrible. "Dap will need to be fed now. I better make sure there is plenty of hay for him in case I have to go to bed." The top of the barn was stacked full so Albert pitched a large quantity into a stall. He returned to the cabin, built up the fire and crawled into bed, freezing and burning with a fever. He never knew when Molly Butcher came home.

CHAPTER SEVEN

Eighteen-year-old Molly Butcher finally reached the snow-covered meadow close to her home a little after dark, exhausted and leading her lame horse. An hour earlier, he had slipped on the ice and sprained his front leg. She dismounted and found he could not have much weight on it. "Sorry, Big Tom, and so near to the barn. Let's see if you can limp on in. I know you are just as tired as I am."

Molly was not only played out, she was in much sorrow. Only a week ago, she had buried her father. A week before he died, a large lion attacked him and would have killed him if she had not shot and scared it off. Badly mauled and bitten, Jim Butcher fought back, hitting the lion with the only thing he could grab. With a large stone, he hammered the lion's head, breaking one of its teeth. Her father did not want to go, but she insisted he go down to Denver, the closest place that could help him. It took five days to get there but he died soon after their arrival.

"I never knew my mother and now my father is gone. What in the world am I to do?" Devastated, the only thing she could think about was to kill the lion that had killed her father. On the way back, she stopped only to let her horse rest and graze a little.

When she entered the barn and lit the lamp, she saw there

was a strange horse in one of the stables. Molly looked him over. "This is a magnificent animal." There was no saddle she could see and wondered if maybe he had wondered in. "No, not with all this hay in his stall." She fed her horse and promised to come back and give him a rubdown as soon as she could. *First, I have to see if someone is in the cabin. I wish there was a window in this house.* Quietly, she opened the door. No sound at first and then a moan as if someone was in pain. But all she saw was coals in the fireplace. She lit the lamp and slowly crossed over to the bed where the sound came from. What she saw was a man with black hair and infected cuts on his forehead; or, were they claw marks resembling those left on her father by the lion. *Oh no, not this again.* She touched his face; it was hot with fever, yet he shook with chills.

Molly was dead tired and she could not think of burying someone else even if it was a stranger. She placed two more blankets on him and bathed his face with cool water. For over four hours, she kept it up until he cooled somewhat. *Now, my turn, just a few minutes.* She stumbled across the room to the other bed and thought about building up the fire as she lay down; it was only a thought.

The crackling fire was a dream; the pan falling on the floor was not. Molly could not move at first. She lay with eyes half open until she regained her senses. "Who are you and what are you doing in my house?"

"Sorry, ma'am. That was an accident, dropping the pan. My name is Albert, and I don't know what I am doing here. Were you the one who sat and bathed my face last night? I thought it was a dream until I saw you this morning. Please don't be afraid. I mean you no harm. I will explain as best I can if you will give me a minute."

Albert did not know where to start or when to stop. From coming to America, to getting sick yesterday, he covered it all without any interruptions from Molly. "May I ask who you are?"

She sat on the side of the bed without any fear of this man, which she thought strange.

"I am Molly Butcher. My father was Jim Butcher. And this is where I live. You say you killed a lion when he attacked you?"

"Yes, his hide is stretched in the barn, his teeth and claws there on the table in a can."

Molly took the piece of broken tooth out, gave a big sigh and started crying. "Thank you so much for killing the monster. I was afraid, but I was going to try and kill him myself. No doubt he is the one who killed my father. This is the tooth he broke when he hit him with a stone. Thank God it's over."

They spent the day sharing events about their lives and caring for their horses. After the evening meal, Molly dressed Albert's wound and went to bed early. He sat tending the fire, thinking of the things that happened the last few weeks. *Were the spirits of the old ones with him or against him? Are they even real? One thing is real for sure and that is Molly. She would be the little girl her uncle White Wolf saw years ago when he came to find his sister. I wonder if she knows he exists? Could I have died from infection if she had not come home? I just thank the Lord she came back. There I am again, thanking the Lord. Does he have anything to do with all of this?*

They both slept late and after the morning chores, Albert wanted Molly to show him the area. Big Tom's leg seemed to be better and Dap was ready to go. The sunshine made the snow sparkle like diamonds. A small herd of deer watched them from across the meadow. The temperature was above freezing and the snow began melting.

"That must be the way you came up," she said, pointing to where he had come through the tunnel. "That's a steep and dangerous trail in the winter."

They rode around the bend and the valley widened out to at least a mile. A waterfall came directly out the side of the mountain and ran its course through the meadow and by the cabin.

They stopped often to admire the scenery.

"What a beautiful place you have here, Molly. What did your father do for a living?"

"We mostly lived off the land. A large garden supplied our vegetables and, of course, there is quite a selection of meat simply walking around. Father trapped and sold the furs to buy the other things we needed. There is plenty of grass for hay to feed the horses. We had two up until two weeks ago. I sold my mare in Denver to pay doctors, but it's okay, I'll get another one."

They turned around and rode in the other direction. It was just as lovely.

"Now I'll show you the root cellar and the garden area, though you can't see much because of the snow."

The garden plot was just a flat place. The root cellar's entrance was a trap door in the floor of the cabin covered with a buffalo hide.

"We keep an oil lamp down there and also in the barn."

Molly went down first and lit the lamp and Albert followed. The room was almost as large as the cabin and filled with all sorts of food in jars and vegetables of all kinds. Cured meats hung from the rafters.

"It stays cold year-round but doesn't freeze. Have you ever seen so much food?"

"No, and I can see what keeps you busy up here."

Before dark, the snow began to fall. They hurried and fed the horses and could hardly see to get back to the cabin. With Albert's help, Molly prepared a big meal from her store of supplies.

"Albert, you said you met my uncle, White Wolf. What is he like?"

"Like any other Indian, I suppose. He is taller than anyone else in his village. He speaks good English and he has a little boy about ten years old. He saw you when you were very young. He came up here to find your mother and found out she was dead. He said the spirits took her because she came up here in the wintertime. He also said he saw a little girl, which must have been you. Why didn't your father take you to meet him?"

"There were hard feelings between them because they married and came up here to live. Father had told them he was looking for gold and the Indians didn't like it."

"Did he ever find any gold?"

"A very small amount. You saw the tunnel he dug off the big one out back. My mother told him they did not need gold, they had each other. After she died, he understood what she meant. I would say I have missed a lot, not having a mother to teach me girl things. Father did his best, but what am I to do now? I don't know anything or anyone else and that's kind of scary."

"I can understand that. I grew up without a father's influence. If it hadn't been for my grandfather talking to me about my future, I would not be here today. I would be back in England with no thought about tomorrow. You know, it's strange the way some things happen. There are so many things I don't understand. What if this cabin would not have been here, if there were not any firewood? What if you were not here to nurse me back to health? Why am I here and why are you here? What strange thing brought us together? Do you believe in the old ones' spirits like your uncle?"

"No, I do not. My father's father was a schoolteacher and a preacher of the gospel, though I never knew him. After he and his wife died, my father came out here to make his fortune. According to what my father said, he sold everything except his father's bible, some written sermons, and a few books. They are in the chest over by my bed. I have read them many times. In fact, they are what I used to learn to read by. Would you care to look at them?"

"I would love to later on. Now, I believe I have enough to think about."

The next morning, Albert left the house early to feed the horses and turn them out into the corral. It was one of the coldest days yet on the mountain, though the creek still was not iced over. "When you boys finish eating, get out there in the sun. Looks like it is going to be a fine day."

He checked the lion skin and it was frozen stiff. Molly was up and breakfast was almost finished when he returned to the cabin. There was a neat stack of papers and a Holy Bible on one end of the table.

"These are the sermons from my grandfather with his Bible and other papers. You are welcome to read them if you like."

"I have to confess, Molly, I have never been a reader. Grandfather's library was filed with all sorts of books and I never took the time to read any of them. The only times I went to church was when I was away to school, then only for something different to do."

"Start with the sermon notes. The scriptures he uses come from the Bible and they are made into an outline he preached from. After reading a couple, you will see what he is doing. There are twenty-four sermons on many subjects. They cover everything from the convicting power of the Holy Spirit, God's plan of salvation, to how we should conduct our lives."

Albert began with the first sermon and it was so interesting he did not notice when Molly finished the dishes and went to bed. He realized it was late when the fire began to die down and it started getting chilly. *These are really good. I wonder if the spirit he talks about is the same spirits the Indians talk about. I'll ask Molly in the morning.*

The fire began to blaze after he placed more wood on the coals. Sleep came soon and so did the new day. The chores became a routine. Albert would tend the horses and Molly did most of the cooking. It became a hassle to get around outside in the snow. He mentioned this to Molly and she went to the root cellar and came back with two pairs of snowshoes.

"This is what we use when the snow gets this deep. I didn't realize it had snowed so much."

Albert had never used them before.

"Just place your foot in the slot and strap it in. With a little practice, it will become easy."

She put her shoes on outside the door and showed him how to walk. He tried and almost fell on his face.

"Start by picking your foot straight up and then move it forward."

He was soon making progress. He was able to walk to the barn and back without hurting himself.

"I feel like Boy, when he tried walking with his wooden leg.

I bet he is running by now."

How deep does the snow usually get up here, Molly?"

"Not over five or six feet deep. A line is stretched from the cabin to the barn in case of a snow blizzard. We hold on to it when we can't see from one place to the other. It is easy to lose direction if there is no line to guide you."

By the time the line was in place, Albert was walking much better.

That afternoon, he asked if the Holy Spirit in the sermons was the same spirits the Indians talked about.

"No, it can't be. The Spirit in the Bible is the Spirit of God. Their spirits are the spirits of the old ones, of their ancestors. I cannot explain it any better. Finish the sermons and then we will study the bible together. Father and I read almost every day and there were some verses neither of us could understand. Maybe we can figure them out."

It was almost dark when someone knocked hard on the door and yelled, "Hello, in the cabin."

Both started for the door. Albert jerked it open and someone fell inside. A heavy buffalo coat weighted him down and a hood covered his head and face. He could not get up. Albert gathered him up as if he were a child and placed him on a chair near the fire.

"Are you hurt, mister?" Molly asked while trying to loosen the coat.

"No, it's this wet buffalo hide and hood that's about to kill me. Can you help me out of this contraption?"

The minute he started to talk, Albert knew who it was, his Uncle Bogie. *It can't be, he could never get here by himself in this kind of weather. The man was unstoppable.* He laughed at the peg-legged man trying to get out of his coat.

"Don't laugh at me, Sonny, or I'll have to teach you some manners in front of this young lady."

"Sorry, Bogie. You just looked so funny flailing around. What in the world are you doing coming up here in this kind of weather?"

"Just a minute, Sonny, first things first. Do you by chance have just a little bit of English tea?"

They both shook their heads no.

"Oh well, coffee maybe?"

Molly started brewing a pot while the men talked.

"Ma'am, you must be Chief White Wolf's niece. If you are, he wants to see you mighty bad, and soon. He thinks he is dying and had a dream that you can keep that from happening. He believes you are his sister's spirit come to live in her daughter. It is confusing to me though you may be able to figure it out. Sonny, your friend, Runner is waiting for us at the foot of this mountain. He thinks the spirits will kill any Indian who comes up here when it snows.

"How did you know Molly and I were up here, Bogie?"

"It was in his dream also. I figured it would be a fifty-fifty chance you would be here and I would get back alive. He was right so far."

"I don't know what I can do for him, but if he thinks I can, it may work. There will be no harm in trying. How bad off is he?"

"I could not tell anything was wrong with him. Three mornings ago, he told me about his dream of death and said you were his only chance to live."

They enjoyed their coffee and decided to wait until morning to leave. Albert asked if it would be alright if he brought the Bible and sermon notes, and was given permission to do so. At daylight, they left the cabin and started their journey down the mountain. Albert and Bogie took turns riding and walking. The only problem, the narrow trail was slick with ice in some places. Runner seemed glad to see all returned safely and more so to start back to his village.

The snow wasn't as deep in the foothills and allowed them to travel faster. They thought the village was deserted when they entered. No one welcomed them nor did they see anyone. They went directly to White Wolf's teepee and entered, Bogie leading them.

"What took you so long?" Boy, asked. "I think his spirit is gone."

No one spoke; they did not know what to say. All was quiet like the rest of the village.

"My spirit is still with me. Is my sister here?"

"I am here, but I am your niece. My mother was your sister."

When she spoke, White Wolf opened his eyes and looked at her.

"You are who you think you are. I think you are my sister. Your voice is hers, and you look exactly like her. Close your eyes and think hard. Don't you remember me? Take your time."

A minute passed, then another. "Yes, I remember you."

"Then I will live because my sister has come home to me."

Boy's face lit up and he hugged everyone in the teepee and went outside yelling, "My Father will live! My Father will live!" The whole village was instantly in a festive spirit; laughing, talking and wanting to see the one who made their chief come back to life.

Plans were made to have a celebration the next day. Several of the braves invited Albert to go on a hunt with them. "We will get the fresh meat," Runner shouted. Albert can kill it a mile away with his gun, and that is what happened, almost.

"Buffalo! Buffalo!" One of the young boys who were out watching the horses came into the village yelling and pointing at three large bulls about four hundred yards away. Most of the people came out to see what the yelling was about. "The spirits have brought them here," Runner exclaimed. "Our chief's sister has brought the spirits with her." All turned to see the woman who had brought the spirits. Molly, frightened by all the attention, went back into the teepee. She was alone with White Wolf. "Don't be afraid, my sister. No one means you any harm. Let us go out and see what is going on."

By this time everyone stood watching the three big bulls. Two were standing in front of the other one and, when they moved, there stood the biggest, a white Buffalo. A gasp sounded from the crowd. "Shoot the white one," someone said excitedly.

"No, not him."

Everyone turned to see who spoke. Molly, who was standing next to White Wolf said, "No," again.

She went to Albert. "You may shoot the other two but not the white one."

"Are you sure it will be alright to kill the other two?"

"Yes, this is why they are here."

Bogie went to where Albert and Molly were.

"Sonny, this is a long shot, but you have to make it from here. You are lucky the wind isn't blowing. Put a little extra powder and use this ball, it's silver and heavier than what you have. Aim a foot higher than where you want to hit him."

Albert sat and rested his elbow on his knees. Slowly, he squeezed the trigger. There was a loud noise and nothing happened. Everyone thought he had missed. Then the buffalo knelt and fell over. He quickly reloaded. The other buffalo never moved. He repeated as before and the animal walked three steps and fell. The white buffalo turned and started walking away. All were in awe at the killing at such a distance. "Blanche," Molly yelled. She turned to Albert and said, "I think I know him." The white buffalo stopped, turned back around and started walking towards Molly who was running to him. When they met, she reached and petted his head and then placed her arms around his neck. There was another gasp from the entire village, which was even louder than the first. The two started again for the village. Halfway there, the buffalo stopped and started pawing through the snow to get to the grass as if nothing had happened. White Wolf motioned for Molly, Albert and Bogie to come with him to his teepee. "We have to talk."

"Tell me, sister, what happened out there? What kind of powers do you have?"

All stood waiting for her answer with anticipation.

"I have no powers, Uncle. This white buffalo stayed the last four winters with my father and I up on the mountain. Father named him Blanche, which means white in French. He stayed in our barn with the horses and ate with them, just a big pet. He is very old and follows other buffalo around to help him get to the grass. I have no special powers."

All except the chief accepted this. "None of the people will never understand or believe what you say. Neither do I. The old ones' spirits are with you." He would not believe her, though he did explain to the people what she said. The two buffalo were made ready for the next day's feast but without the festive spirit they had before. Not much talking went on that evening in the chief's teepee.

The day of the celebration, the white buffalo continued to

feed close to the village. Everyone distanced themselves from it and Molly. White Wolf said they were afraid the spirits would be angry with them if they said or even thought something wrong.

Boy and Singing Dove would be the first to approach Molly. She and Albert were sitting by themselves discussing their situation when Boy approached them.

"Would you like to see what I can do with my new leg?"

"Yes, we would," Albert answered.

He ran a hundred yards and back very fast. When he was near them he jumped, turned a flip, and landed upright. "This is what Uncle Bogie taught me. It still hurts a little, but not as much as before. Soon I will have a race with Runner."

"That was amazing. I can't believe you have gotten this good in such a short time," Albert said.

Molly knew Boy wanted to ask her something. "What is it you want to know?"

"Are you just a person like anyone else? My father says you are not."

"I am a regular woman, Boy. No different than any other woman. All that has happened, though it does seem strange, has a logical answer." Again, she related the story about the white buffalo being a pet and she was White Wolf's niece, nothing more. "I am not the spirit of my mother or anyone else. Only the Spirit of God can do the things impossible for us to do. Albert and I are studying about that now. Would you like to study with us?"

"Yes, but someone wants to talk with you." He motioned to a beautiful woman about Molly's age who came and sat as Albert and Boy excused themselves.

"You must be Singing Dove," Molly stated.

"Yes, how do you know? Are you a spirit woman?"

"No, I am not," she returned with a sighing gesture. "Just a woman like you. Albert told me about a beautiful young woman who made his remarkable coat and you fit his description, that's all." Singing Dove was more at ease after this statement. She explained to Molly she was not of this tribe. White Wolf's father had taken her in as a little girl when her wandering tribe came by. There was no one who wanted to be responsible for raising her after her mother died. "I lived with him until he built me a place of my own three years ago. If you want, you can come and live with me. I know it must be hard to stay in one room with four men."

This was a dream come true for Molly. "I will gladly take you up on your offer. They probably are uncomfortable with a woman living with them. Show me where you live and I will tell White Wolf what we are doing."

The two women moved Molly's few belongings into Singing Dove's teepee. There were wall-to-wall buffalo skins that had been softened by many hours of hard work. Hides fastened on both sides of the teepee poles made it easier to keep warm. A bed of blankets lay on one side of the room and several more were folded and stacked neatly on the other side. "This is what I do in my spare time. I weave blankets for those who can't do it for themselves. Help yourself to as many as you want."

"You have things fixed so nice. Where did you get all of these soft skins on the floor?"

"I am not yet married, and there is no shortage of young hunters in this and other villages who want to change that. What about you? Is Albert your man?"

"No, I have no man. Albert is just a friend."

Molly told the story of how she found him sick in her cabin

after her father had died.

"Would you be offended if I told you I find him very attractive?"

"No, though I have to say I also think he is very attractive and he is a good, honest person. Albert is searching for something, coming all the way from England thinking he might find it here."

A loud commotion brought the girls out of the teepee. Bogie was leading the white buffalo with Boy riding on his back.

"This should be proof enough he is not a spirit buffalo," Bogie called out to the girls. "Now we have to change their minds about you being your mother's spirit."

The people were beginning to think differently and all enjoyed the celebration, except for White Wolf who refused to believe Molly was not his sister's spirit.

The celebration quickly came to an abrupt end mid-afternoon when dark ominous clouds began rolling over the mountains. The Indians, knowing what was in store for them, started gathering the food and other objects, bringing them into their dwellings. White Wolf sent Runner to get the boys who were watching the herd of horses. "This will be a bad storm," he said to Albert. "The spirits from the mountains are not pleased."

Within a few minutes everyone had settled in their teepees as blizzard winds and snow pounded the village. White Wolf began chanting prayers to his gods. Albert, Bogie, and Boy watched as he took something from his leather pouch and threw it in the fire. A thick smoke ascended and went out the smoke hole. He stopped long enough to ask why they were not praying to their gods. Albert remembered the last of the sermon outlines was about a storm. He unfolded the leather wrap and found the one he wanted. It was entitled, "Why Worry About the Storms."

He read aloud the story of when Jesus caused a storm to cease.

"Matthew 8:23, and when he was entered into a ship, his disciples followed him. And, behold, there arose a great tempest in the sea, insomuch that the ship was covered with the waves: but he was asleep. And his disciples came to him, and awoke him, saying, Lord, save us: we perish. And he saith unto them, Why are ye fearful, O ye of little faith? Then he arose, and rebuked the winds and the sea; and there was a great calm. But the men marveled, saying, What manner of man is this, that even the winds and the sea obey him!"

"Who was this man who could do such a thing?" White Wolf asked. "Is he a god?"

"I haven't got all the answers yet, but the Bible calls him Jesus, the Son of God. I wish Molly were here. She knows much more than I do."

"Do you know what a 'little faith' is?" Boy asked.

"I understand it to be what one believes. You believe something is true because the person that tells you doesn't lie. This is the best I can explain it. We will ask Molly later. Do you want to hear more of what is in these notes?" Boy was eager to know, though White Wolf and Bogie did not answer.

"Psalm 27:1, The Lord is my light and my salvation; whom shall I fear? the Lord is the strength of my life; of whom shall I be afraid? Psalm 27:3, Though a host should encamp against me, my heart shall not fear. He goes on to say if we believe in this God, we have no need to be afraid of anything because he watches over them that trust in him. Another time we will talk about this."

While they were talking the worst of the storm had passed and there was just a light flurry of snow. Boy was the first to realize the storm had blown itself out. "Look," he said excitedly, "the storm is over." They all went outside where others were gathered. "Look what Albert's God did." No one understood what he was talking about, except those who heard the story from the sermon notes.

Molly and Singing Dove were fast becoming friends. Molly never had another woman to talk to or share her feelings with, only a father, who never understood the needs and upbringing of his daughter. Many of their discussions were about the young men in their village. "My father always said, 'Marriage is a lifelong commitment, only death could separate the two.' What do you think, Singing Dove?"

"This is the same as we believe, though a few don't pay much mind to it. Some men think it is alright to have more than one wife and some women go from one teepee to another. These are never happy, and after a while, no one will have anything to do with them."

"You are interested in Albert. Why don't you tell him so?" Molly stated one evening.

"He is never by himself. There are always others around him."

"I may be able to help. Let's cook for him tomorrow. I will leave and you can be by yourself with him."

The invitation was given and Albert accepted with no idea he was being set up.

A good meal was prepared and Albert arrived on time to eat with the two most beautiful women in the village.

"You sit and Singing Dove will fix your plate. We have cooked so much I am going to share with the men. I will be right back."

Molly left with two pots of food and never returned. Albert and Singing Dove ate and talked about casual things. Then he began to show signs of uneasiness.

"Singing Dove, there is something I would like to talk to you about. I don't know how to say what's on my mind."

"Take a deep breath like you were going to squeeze a trigger and say what is on your mind." She was thinking this is going to be easier than she imagined.

"It's about Molly. Do you think she would marry me if I asked her? I know you are her best friend. Would you feel her out and let me know how she feels?"

It was a while before Singing Dove could speak. She turned to wipe the tears from her eyes before Albert could see them. Quickly, she composed herself and stated she would see what she could find out.

"I loved her from the first moment I saw her. I had a high fever and she bathed my face with cool water. I thought she was an angel and I have thought of nothing much since. I don't know how to tell her this. I was excited when I saw an opportunity to talk to you alone."

"Tell her what you told me and she will let you know her heart's feelings, and I hope the best for you both. Now go."

Albert was determined to do as Singing Dove suggested, and now had to be the time. He opened the flap to the teepee where Molly sat talking to her uncle and asked to speak with her. She was shaking and felt weak as she walked out with him. "Are you cold? You are shaking like a leaf. Here, take my coat." He placed it around her shoulder but it did not help.

"I have been talking to Singing Dove and I have something to say to you. I have spoke my heart to her and now I will do the same with you."

What have I done? Molly thought. *He is forever lost to me.* She began to wobble and Albert caught her and held her in his arms. "This will only take a minute then I will take you home. I want to marry you, Molly. I love you and want you to be my wife."

She fainted.

Albert was scared at this point. He whisked her up and ran to Singing Dove's teepee. He called out and she opened the entrance for him. "Something happened to Molly. Can you help her?" He explained as he sat her down.

"You go back to your place and give me a few minutes alone with her. She will be alright. Come back in an hour."

The hour was slow to pass. When he entered their teepee again, both girls were laughing and talking as if nothing had happened.

"Are you alright, Molly?" Was all he could think to say.

"Yes, I am fine, and yes, I will marry you, Albert Anderson, if you still want me."

All of this happened so fast he was unable to say anything more. "Go home, Albert, and come back in the morning. Everyone may be in their right mind by then."

Sleep was impossible for Albert that night. Just before daylight, he dozed off to be awakened by the smell of food. The girls brought two meals a day for the men.

"Wake up, Albert." It was the voice of Singing Dove. "There is much to do today if you and Molly are to be married."

"What is this?" Bogie asked, getting excited. "You finally asked sweet Molly, and did she really say yes?"

Albert ran his fingers through his now long black hair that he usually braided like the Indians. He motioned for Molly. "I did ask her to be my wife and she agreed. Now we would like to ask for her uncle's permission." White Wolf stood straight, folded his arms across his chest and with his authority as chief answered, "I give my permission to this brave white Englishman to marry my sister's daughter." That was all he said.

Molly wanted to have a Christian wedding. "There is one of my grandfather's sermon outlines that explains how to do it." She looked through the sermons and found it, then asked Bogie if he would read and preform the wedding.

"I am not a licensed preacher, but if it is your wish, I will be glad to do it."

"It's not the license that counts, it's the way God would have it done, and if Albert doesn't mind, this is what I want."

"There are two things I want, Molly. The first and most important one is we marry; the second is we spend the rest of the winter in your cabin on the mountain."

"Our cabin, Albert. From now on, we are one as the Word says and all we have belongs to both of us."

The sun was shining bright and the wedding took place that morning so the new married couple could return to their cabin, hopefully before another winter storm came. The whole village turned out to watch this Christian wedding. Molly and Albert stood facing each other and Bogie, dressed in his new, almost white, leather clothes, stood before them with the wedding outline in his hand. He folded it and handed it back to Molly. "I don't need this to marry the two people I love the most. You both know you are standing before God and he is watching. Molly, do you want to marry my nephew, Albert, more than anything else? Do you promise to love him and care for him as long as you live?"

"Yes, I promise, knowing God is watching."

"What about you, Albert? do you make this same promise?"

"I make this same promise, Uncle, for as long as I live."

"Well, that's it. You two will be Mr. and Mrs. Anderson for

the rest of your lives. You can kiss her now and make sure you come back down when the grass turns green again.

The young married couple left within the hour, happier than ever before, though not knowing what lay ahead. And that is the way it should be.

CHAPTER EIGHT

"What if the horses are not able to climb the narrow trail, Albert? I never thought about that before we left?"

"I thought about it, but things have been working in our favor so far, maybe this will also."

The journey to the narrow ledge trail was without incident. The snow, only about a foot deep, allowed them to make good time.

"Someone must be watching over us, sweet heart," Albert stated when they came to the trail. "If we can get past this, the rest of the way should be a cinch." They dismounted and led the horses until the trail turned and the danger was behind them. The snow, being deeper as they climbed higher, began to slow their progress, though Big Tom, Molly's horse, seemed not to have any trouble breaking his way through. They reached the place where Albert had camped when he came up the first time. The shelter under the overhang was large enough to accommodate them and their horses.

"If the weather holds out, we should reach the cabin late tomorrow, then we will be able to start living a normal life together, Molly, darling. So much has happened since I spent the night here only weeks ago."

Daylight found them well on their way. A cloud settled over the mountain and made it hard to see very far. "Do you know your way, Molly?"

"I can't see a thing to tell me where I am, but Big Tom must know. He keeps pulling on the reins like he wants to lead the way. Should we trust him?"

"I don't think we have a choice. It could stay like this for days but I am willing to take a chance if you are."

Big Tom had lived all his life on the mountain. Jim Butcher bought him as a colt twelve years ago and used him for every kind of work that was needed. He was three hundred pounds heavier than Dap who weighed over a thousand pounds. The two to three-foot-deep snow did not slow him. Molly let the reigns slack and allowed Big Tom to choose the direction. For two hours, they plowed on. Then the cloud began to break and the sun could be seen at intervals.

"We must be getting above the clouds," Molly stated. "I know where we are now."

By the time they reached the cabin, darkness had settled in. Albert tended the horses and Molly volunteered to prepare a hearty meal. The rope line from the barn to the cabin came in handy in the dark. A couple hours later with the cabin warming, they enjoyed the best meal in several days.

"Molly, tell me about yourself. I know very little about you and you know nothing about me. Hopefully we will have many years to share together, but I want to know about your life here on the mountain with your father."

"My mother died when I was born and father was all I ever knew the first years of my life. We would go down to Denver two or three times a year to get supplies and when I was older, I met several people I could talk to. Mrs. Johns ran a boarding house where we would stay. She was the one who helped me the most with 'girl things' as she called it. I actually stayed with her and helped with the cooking for her customers during the last three summers. Father taught me to read, write, and do my sums, and I have several books which also helped a lot. Singing Dove was the first girl my age I ever had as a friend. She taught me a lot about things I didn't know, especially about the opposite sex. She was in love with you, Albert; we planned that evening to get you alone with her so she could tell you. I didn't know until then I loved you myself and I thought I would die when you came to tell me you wanted to marry me. I just knew you was going to tell me it was her you loved."

"Molly, my love, from the moment I saw you I felt you would be mine. So many things have happened the last year and a half which cannot be explained. I hadn't thought about my future until Grandfather asked me questions I could not answer. Those questions started a fire within me and it's still there. I met Uncle Bogie, a man I didn't know existed. He told me about America and I had to come here. All the way from England to the east coast of this great land, then over a thousand miles to where we met your Uncle White Wolf and his little tribe. It is as if some great power is directing me where to go. I had no choice; it brought me here to your cabin on this mountain where I found you. I cannot believe these things just happened. Is it the old ones' spirits, or is it God? I have to read your sermons and the Bible. What I'm looking for is there. I can feel it. Please help me to understand. I love you with all my heart, Molly, and together we will figure this thing out."

For the next three weeks, the snow continued to fall. The rope line from cabin to barn was raised four feet to keep it above the snow. Two times each day, Albert tended the horses.

"Thanks to Mr. Butcher, Dap old boy, we have enough hay and grain for several weeks. I have to learn to plan ahead as he did. It takes all summer to prepare for the harsh winters we have this high on the mountain."

When the morning chores were done, Albert and Molly poured over the sermon outlines until he could recite them word for word. He compiled other scripture related to what was already there. Before going to bed, they read the Bible and talked about what it meant to them. After three weeks of studying, Molly asked, "Have these last weeks reading and discussion given you any satisfaction as to what you are looking for?"

"I feel more at peace than I ever have, my love. I only wish I could have experienced this earlier in my life. Do you think there would be any way we could leave here for a few days and go to where there is a church? I would like to talk to a preacher.

I have so many questions and so many things I want to know."

"Sorry to disappoint you, Albert, that is impossible with all this snow. Maybe we can go in five or six weeks when winter eases up. Until then, we will continue to read, study, and talk about the Bible like Father and I used to do. Albert, you spoke to me about your mother and father and I can sympathize with you, but you never speak of your grandparents."

"Grandfather was always gone when I was growing up. I was a little afraid of him the few times I saw him. He seemed very stern and never spoke to me as a small boy. He retired a few years ago and moved back to his castle. That is when I came to know him. I found he is a lonely old man and nothing like I thought he was. I saw my grandmother only a couple of times. Mother said they didn't want us around and I should never go and see them. Now I know she lied to me. It was her that didn't want me to know them. When I asked Grandfather about her, tears showed in his eyes. He said he lost the only thing of any real value to him when she died. He explained he was so involved with his job, he wasted his life doing what he thought was important. He regretted what he did but it was then too late. 'When you find your love, Albert, be sure and not do like I did. Love her and be a husband to her every day because life is short and you will regret it if you don't.' That is what he told me and I intend to do exactly that, my love."

"That is about the saddest thing I have ever heard. I hope someday I can meet him. Do you think it would be possible?"

"There is nothing I would rather do than have you and Grandfather meet. I know he would love you as much as I do darling."

They talked the evening away, like they usually did, about their past life and their hopes for the future. Albert, praying whatever was guiding him would continue to show him the way and Molly assuring him it would.

Though mostly isolated by the deep snow, there were a few days they were able, with their snowshoes, to get in some walking. Albert exercised as often as possible and hiking uphill with snowshoes was quite a challenge. Since leaving England over a year ago, he had grown from a grown boy to a hardened man. His strength and endurance was unbelievable. He braided his long black hair like the Indians but kept his beard trimmed and neat. The horses were also kept in shape by workouts in the deep snow.

"This will be a good day to climb the mountain," Molly said one morning a few weeks later. "If we can make the top, we will be able to see if the snow is melting down in the foothills. Winter isn't over yet, though it won't be long now. I would guess it to be the middle or last of February."

The horses were anxious to be ridden and Big Tom wanted to be in the lead. Molly packed a picnic lunch for the ride which would take all day. There was not much of a trail, but Molly had made this trip so many times she needed none. The snow was packed so hard the horses seldom broke through. "Never have I seen a prettier place than this," Albert stated when they stopped to rest the horses. "I wish Father and Grandfather could see this."

After three hours of steady climbing, Molly pointed toward the east. "Look, Albert. This is what I wanted to show you."

He looked and could not believe what he saw. There was no snow at the bottom of the mountain; just green, everything was a green carpet. "How can it be? There are four to five feet of snow here and it looks like summer time down there. When will we be able to travel safely down the mountain?" he asked excitedly.

"Three to four weeks if there is not a major blizzard. If there is, no one knows. Winter could last until May or later."

"I hope it will be soon. There is so much I want to do down there and we will have to get back here to plant a garden, cut firewood, gather hay for the horses and a lot of other things. Our first winter was great and I cannot wait till summer gets here." Albert was as excited as a little kid and Molly was happy for him.

"Let's eat lunch and plan what we are going to do next," she advised.

For the next week, Albert could not contain himself. Up early and late to bed, writing notes of things he wanted to do when summer came. "What would you want most if you had a wish, love?" he asked one morning.

"I would like at least one glass window in this cabin so I could see out. Father intended to get one but it never happened."

"I have three hundred dollars left from what Grandfather gave me when I left England. It should be enough for a while. Make a list of what we need for the coming year and that will be one of the first things we do. How did you haul everything up here?"

"The man who owns the store brought it up with pack mules and wagon. Of course, the oats and corn will be later on in the year unless he has some left over from last year. We save our seed from year to year, and as far as I know, we don't need equipment of any kind, just the usual like sugar, salt, and other things we cannot raise."

They waited the three weeks and decided to try and check out the narrow mountain pass. There was a small amount of snow on the pass but no ice. They slowly made their way down without any problems. "Our angels are still watching over us, Molly, my love. I cannot wait to tell Uncle Bogie and our Indian friends about God and the other things we have been studying about."

"I would not go too far with that if I were you. There are some who don't want to hear it, and others will get offended. Let the Holy Spirit lead you and it will work out. Not all people are able to deal with this as you are, so go slow. Feel White Wolf out before you talk to him about God. You know he believes in the spirits of the old ones and if you push too hard, he or the others may never listen to you."

Albert thought about what Molly said and agreed she was right, and if he could restrain his self, he would.

"Look, there are some of White Wolf's band, Molly." Five Indians were a hundred yards away riding in their direction. He started to wave and greet them when Molly stopped him. "Those are Comanche. Looks like a hunting party but they will take a scalp any time. Keep your rifle trained on the one with the three feathers. He is the one to watch. Whatever happens, don't show any fear, just smile. I will shoot first if need be. You shoot the one with the feathers."

The Indians stopped and started talking among themselves and making gestures.

"If they start to spread apart shoot because they will attack. If they stay in a bunch, we will wait."

They stayed in a group and walked their horses slowly toward Molly and Albert.

"They want our horses and your gun. Mine is hidden and they won't expect me to have one. We are being tested so show no fear."

The Indians stopped and the largest one rode close to Albert and motioned for his rifle. Albert shook his head no and laughed, all the while pointing his rifle at the one with the feathers.

"We come from the old spirits and the white man's God with a message for White Wolf. They will be angry if you do not let us pass," Molly spoke.

For a moment, they did not say or do anything. Then the one next to Albert raised his spear and held it close to Albert's chest and again motioned for the rifle. Albert smiled and said no.

All at once, there was an explosion and the spear was torn from the Indian's hand.

"Laugh, Albert," Molly yelled as she jumped to the ground and started chanting and patting her chest. Albert threw back his head and roared with laughter. The Indians, not knowing what was happening, turned in fear and ran until they were out of sight.

"That was a good shot, Molly! Did you see his eyes when you shot the spear out of his hand?"

"I didn't shoot, it was..."

"It was my fancy shooting, Sonny. A very good shot if I say

so myself."

Bogie stepped from behind a boulder and they all had a big laugh.

"Molly, what in the world were you doing?" Albert asked.

"Just singing the Comanche death song."

"After what happened, every Comanche within a hundred miles will think you to be messengers from the old ones. I would say by the time this story, with its embellishments, is spread, you will not have any more trouble with them," Bogie declared.

News of what happened since they saw each other last was shared on their ride to the village. Bogie announced he was treated like an equal to the chief, and Boy could run, jump and hold his own with any of the other children. Bogie said with a big smile, "Boy cannot run as fast as Runner, but he sure gives him a challenge."

In turn, Albert spoke of his consuming desire to study and to share the Word of God with others. The news that Molly and Albert were coming, reached the village before they did, and everyone gathered with Chief White Wolf in front of his teepee for a grand welcome. Bogie told the story about the confrontation with the Comanche as the people stood spellbound and completely silent. There was always a fear of the warring Comanche nation and to hear of them running instead of fighting was unbelievable. When the greeting ended, Molly went with Singing Dove to her place and Albert to White Wolf's. Boy, being very excited, told Albert they had a good surprise for him. White Wolf said the surprise could wait till later because now was the time to listen to their friend tell his stories of living on the mountain.

"I have to say, sir, the best thing that has ever happened to me was to come to America. I know now it has been the hand of God that led me here to find you and your people who welcomed Uncle Bogie and me into your homes and hearts. That in itself could not have been an accident. Then came the greatest thing of all, I found your niece who introduced me to

God. I now have what I have been searching for and am content. Except, I feel a need to share the Lord with all who will listen, especially my friends here. If you and your people want to learn about God, I will be glad to teach you what I know. You speak of the spirits of the old ones and I do not say you are wrong. I believe the Holy Spirit of God was here before man ever existed. Let me know if you want to hear more about him."

"You have grown," Bogie exclaimed after Albert made his statement. "Not only physically, but in many other ways. I am glad you have found what you came here to find. I have also found what I always wanted, friends who have made me a part of their family. This is something I never had before we came here and I do not intend to ever leave. I give you all that is mine back in England. When you go back, tell your Grandfather thanks for convincing me to come here with you."

"I may go back to visit, Bogie, though like you, I feel this is where I belong."

White Wolf said he would listen later to what Albert had to say about the spirits but now they would celebrate their return. Boy went to get Molly and Singing Dove and gathered everyone in front of the chief's teepee. When all were assembled, White Wolf spoke. "We are glad to have Albert and my sister's daughter here with us again." The Chief pointed to a new teepee next to his. "Everyone helped in some way to build this for you. It is yours and we hope to have you with us always."

Albert and Molly, in turn, gave their thanks for what was given them. "We wondered where we would stay. Thank each of you so much." All waited outside while they went in to see the inside. "Another blessing from God," Albert said.

Blankets and soft buffalo hides covered the floor and more were neatly stacked in the back. Everything they needed was in its place. "Your uncle is making it hard for us to leave here and go back to our cabin," Albert said.

"I know, but we must, it is our home for now. Who but God knows what will be in our future."

A hunt was planned for the next day's celebration. That evening, several women, led by Singing Dove, prepared a large meal for the visitors. Again, thanks were given and the two were left alone to enjoy their food and their first night in their new home. By the time Albert and Molly were up, the hunting party had left. Albert was a little disappointed to have missed the hunt so Molly suggested they go for a ride and asked Boy if he would go to where the horses were grazing and bring Big Tom and Dap back. "Can I go with you?" he wanted to know.

"If your father doesn't care, it will be fine with us."

He was given permission and was soon back, riding his pony and leading theirs. The prairie was in profuse bloom with flowers of all colors. The small river running rapidly over the rocks made a soothing sound and Boy never ceased his chatter. He was happy he could go riding with two such special people. They were five miles from the village when they rounded a bend in the river. A huge ponderosa pine spread its branches wide and Molly asked if they might stop and let the horses graze on the succulent grass and rest for a few minutes. While they sat and talked, Boy went to the river to try and catch minnows.

"When will we be able to start planting our garden?" Albert asked. Molly was answering his question when they heard Boy yell. They both ran in the direction where they heard the call for help. Something hit Albert and he fell headlong and unconscious. As he fell, four strong Indians grabbed Molly and two others had Boy already with his hands tied. Molly fought like a tiger but was soon overcome by the four stronger men. She tried to see how bad off Albert was while being dragged quickly towards the horses. Big Tom and Boy's pony was easily caught but Dap pulled loose and ran back towards the village. The six Indians wasted no time in tying Molly and Boy to their horses and leaving the area. Molly soon saw she could not escape and asked Boy if he was alright.

"Yes, are you?"

Molly confirmed she was, and began to silently pray. *Lord*

please let Albert be alright and keep Boy and me safe.

It was long after dark when they stopped to sleep and let the horses graze. Molly and Boy, with their hands and feet tied, were guarded by two of the Indians while the other four slept.

CHAPTER NINE

Dap entered the village thirty minutes after the incident, all lathered with sweat and a white foam from the fast running knowing something terrible had happened. He stopped in front of White Wolf's dwelling and let out a loud squeal. Soon the whole village had assembled around Dap, who continued to make nervous sounds. The hunting party was still out, which consisted of most of the young men.

"Something is bad wrong," Bogie stated to the Chief.

"I know, my friend. I believe this horse wants to show us something." Then he spoke to the crowd and named eight men besides Bogie and himself. "Get your horses and weapons, quick. There may have been an accident or foul play. We must be prepared." Then he spoke to one of the other men. "Go try and find the hunters, tell them what you know. They can follow us."

The group was ready in a short time and had to ride hard to keep up with Dap.

There could have been an accident, Bogie thought, *though I don't think so. Not with all three of them missing. If someone else is involved, they will surely pay.*

Dap stopped under the large pine where he had fought to get away from those who tried to capture him. Bogie, first to dismount, found several items Molly and Albert left when Boy yelled his alarm. "Scatter out and be alert. Let us know if you find anything."

Bogie was rubbing Dap, trying to soothe him when someone called out. They had found Albert.

Everyone immediately gathered around him. He was as he fell, face down, his head in a puddle of blood.

"Albert is dead," one of the older men commented.

"No, not yet," Bogie answered. "I can feel a slight pulse."

They found the weapon not far away. A stone hatchet, thrown by someone, had found its mark. A four-inch gash across his forehead at the hairline revealed the white skull.

"Now is the time to tend his wound while he is unconscious," Bogie informed. Out of a small leather medicine bag he always wore around his neck, Bogie took a needle and with a long hair from a horse's tail he sewed up the gash. White Wolf informed the men not to walk around and disturb the area. "Wait till the hunters get here. They will find the trail."

"You take our friend back to the village, Bogie. I will wait for the others to get here," White Wolf said. Bogie mounted Dap and Albert was placed in front of him in the saddle. Slowly they made their way home. From a distance, the village people saw them coming and ran to meet them, asking questions which could not be answered. Albert was placed in his teepee and Bogie asked Singing Dove to get someone to come help him with Albert.

Soon the story was spread throughout the village and so did all sorts of speculation as to what might have taken place, and the vigil began.

When the hunting party arrived early that afternoon and was told about the incident, they eagerly caught up fresh mounts. The women would process the meat that was brought in, though the celebration would be postponed. Bogie said he would go with them because there was nothing else he could do here. While waiting for them, White Wolf worked out the trail the renegade Indians had taken. The hatchet used to try and kill Albert was made by the Comanche and this caused much concern for the Utes. They were not hated enemies, though not on the best terms either. "We won't jump to any conclusions. Just be ready for anything and hope for the best," Bogie commented.

The trail was not hard to follow. Runner, a good friend of Albert, led the band along the creek until it was too dark to see. As much as they wanted to go on, White Wolf called a halt for the day.

"We cannot afford to lose their trail. If they turn in another direction, time will be lost trying to find it again." Runner reported there were eight horses in all, two being Molly's and Boy's, the other six, Comanche. "That doesn't sound like a raiding party," said White Wolf. "Why did they not capture Albert along with the others?"

"When we find them, I will personally ask why," Bogie harshly stated. "If Albert don't make it, these six men will surely die by my hand."

No fire was built that night in case the ones they were hunting would see it and be more alert.

Two sentries were placed on guard so there would not be any surprises. Bogie spent the night thinking and wondering about Albert. *Lord, I don't know much about praying. I guess you already know one of your followers is in bad shape. If I could ask you a question, it would be, "Why did you let this happen to someone who loved you so? Molly and a little innocent boy are in the hands of six savages and I pray you will let us find them before something bad happens. Amen.*

****

Molly and Boy were allowed to drink the next morning, though no one ate. There was much discussion about Boy. Some thought he should die, others said to keep him alive and the woman would be easier to handle. They asked Boy several things trying to find out if he understood what they were talking about. He acted as though he did not understand what they were saying. He talked to Molly in English, which they did not understand. He called them some very bad names and, if they had known, they would have beaten him severely.

"Do you know why they have taken us prisoner?"

"No. They think you are some kind of spirit woman, though, and some of them are afraid of you. The one who is in charge says your husband was the one they should have taken. Your power with the spirits is not strong. He said he heard you sing their death song a few days ago and he was not afraid."

"He must be part of those who confronted us when we came off the mountain. Bogie shot the spear out of his hand and they thought Albert had done something. They all ran, him included."

They followed the creek at a brisk speed whenever they could. Then, leaving the creek, they went south and then west, back towards the mountains stopping only to drink and rest the horses for a few minutes. When dark came, they built a small fire in a ravine and gave Molly and Boy a little food for the first time. The one who brought it said his name was Raven and wanted them to say his name, which they did. It made him smile. He was the one who seemed to be in charge. They were not tied that night but two men never took their eyes off them. Molly knelt and prayed before going to sleep and once when she awoke during the night. "Lord, please let Albert be alright and keep Boy and me safe. I don't understand why this is happening and I know you are in complete control. Amen." Then she hummed a hymn. The guards, she could tell, were frightened when she did this.

Early in the morning, Boy placed his hand on her shoulder and softly shook her. The Comanche were standing watching when she opened her eyes. "Don't act like you are afraid, Molly. The guards have been telling them about your praying and chanting last night."

"I am not afraid, Boy. The Lord is with us and I will show them." She went directly to Raven and shook her finger at him. As she raised her hands to the sky, she said, "My God is the creator of all things, including the mountains and even you." She then poked him in the chest. He stepped back as she did. Kneeling, she prayed, "Lord, again I ask you to be with Albert and Boy. Help us to be strong in the time of our trouble." Then she began to sing a hymn. The Indians began talking and pointing at her, the sky and the mountains.

"It is them who are afraid of you, Molly," Boy said under his breath. "They believe you are talking to the spirits of the old ones who live in the high mountains."

"I talk to the one who made the old ones and the high mountains. It is he who is in charge, not them."

"Can I talk to them? I speak and understand their tongue. I can say you gave me this power."

"Not yet. We will see what they have in mind first."

The course they took brought them around the foot of the mountain and back north, the way they had come only on the other side of the mountain. They rode the horses slower and did not stop till late afternoon. Two of the Indians were gathering wood for a fire when one of them yelled. The others ran to see what happened and saw a large rattlesnake close to his foot. It was coiled and ready to strike again. Boy was close and he flipped with his show-off trick and landed with his wooden leg crushing the snake's head. Even the one who was bitten looked amazed at his action. The snake had struck the Indian on the upper arm when he stooped to pick up a piece of wood. It was Raven's younger brother. He suffered immensely, all the while asking that the prisoners be set free. "This is a bad omen," he cried. Before midnight, the young man was dead.

When morning came, they dug a shallow trench, wrapped him in his blanket and buried him.

"We will do as my brother asked," Raven declared. "You are free and we will take you back home."

Boy repeated this in English. Molly took Raven's hand in her own. "I am sorry you lost your brother, and if I can do anything for you, just ask." Again, Boy translated.

"If you know the spirits of the old ones, ask them to look after him. It is enough."

"I will ask my God to do just that."

"I will tell him what you said, Molly." Boy began to talk and Raven did not take his eyes off Molly until he finished speaking.

"Tell her I am the one who killed her man. I am sorry also."

"He is not dead, Raven. You will see."

Before dark, Boy pointed to a cloud of dust in the distance. "Someone comes and there are many."

The two groups met and Raven's party was quickly surrounded.

Albert was the first to dismount and then Molly was in his arms. "I knew you were alive. God told me you were, Albert."

There were twenty Utes, including White Wolf, and as many Comanche.

"You and your men will die, Raven," Red Cloud, the Comanche Chief, spoke loud with disgust. "Why did you do this to our friends?"

The story was soon told. A white man wanted Albert dead and his wife brought to him along with his long rifle. He would be waiting for them in their cabin on the mountain. In return, he would give the Comanche twenty rifles with plenty powder and shot. "We would never have to fear our enemies again," he said.

"You will die for such a thing," Chief Red Cloud said again.

"No," Albert exclaimed, "no killing. My God will have his way in this and no one has to die. Molly and I will talk to our God and he will show us what to do. Leave us alone with Raven and his men."

Two camps were set up a little distance apart. Boy was to translate.

"I am the one who tried to kill you and you are not angry?" Raven asked.

"No, I am not angry with you. What good would it do if you were to die? Maybe you have learned a lesson from this and you can do good from now on."

Molly related the story of their capture all the way to the death of Raven's brother from the snakebite and him asking to set them free.

"This God you talk about, is he only for the white man?"

"He is for all who believe in him. Jesus is his name."

Albert spoke of his growing up in another country, coming here to America and of the things that happened since he came. He hoped Boy could translate properly and they could grasp some of what was said.

"We will talk of this later. Now I must see what my chief requires of me."

Red Cloud said he would talk to his people and see what they say before making a decision.

"What are we going to do about the man who started this mess, the man now waiting at your cabin?" Bogie asked on the way back to the village.

"If he is still there when we go up, we will decide then. Maybe he would like to work for us. There is no real harm done."

"No real harm done? You can't see that gash in your forehead. A half-inch deeper and you wouldn't be here now. You have sure changed since you climbed the mountain, Sonny."

"It's not the mountain that changed me Bogie. The Lord and Holy Spirit is what changed me."

Bogie could see a complete transformation in his nephew and wondered if this change could come into his life. Not that he wanted it to happen, not now anyway.

The postponed celebration took place the day after they returned to the village. None of the people could understand why Albert refused to punish the ones who tried to kill him. He reasoned, "They have been punished enough. Raven lost his brother because of what they had done. Just forget this and enjoy our celebration. Molly and I will be going to our home on the mountain in three weeks."

The time passed quickly. The village women planted their seeds for this year's crops and Albert, for the first time, helped plant a garden.

"This is women's work," Runner stated one morning when Albert chose to work in the fields instead of going on a hunt with the men.

"I already know about hunting, my friend. This farming is new to me. You can use my rifle if you like."

When Albert made this offer, Runner's eyes lit up and he yelled, "Yippee," forgetting about his friend doing women's work.

"I'll be up in a couple of weeks and help you do the women's work, Sonny," Bogie promised when Albert and Molly were packed and ready to leave.

"You are such a good friend, Bogie," Molly said, and hugged him. "We can use all the help we can get."

The three-day trip was without incident. However, on the third day, a huge grizzly caused a two-hour delay. "I believe this is the same bear I saw the first time I came up here. White Wolf said they will sometimes circle around and attack from the rear."

He ambled off looking for grubs and they continued their journey to the cabin. They entered the meadow and all the snow was gone except where the sun never touched. Dap started to get nervous and looking towards the south, shook his head. Something was on the ground a few hundred yards away. They decided to check it out before going on to the cabin.

"It's your friend, the white buffalo, Molly. It looks like he's been shot."

They dismounted to get a closer look. "You are right, Albert, and look at his right horn. It looks covered with blood. After searching the area and not finding anything, they started for the cabin.

Someone was lying on the floor in front of the fireplace wrapped in a blanket. Hurriedly, Molly lit the lamp.

"He is dead," Albert said, "and for several days I would say."

Molly picked up a note from the table.

"His name is Claude," she said and continued to read. "I always heard a white Buffalo was sacred and I guess they are. I just shot one and when I went to take his skin, he gored me. Always, I took what I wanted and never cared for other people.

I am a dead man now and ask, when you find me, bury me and say a prayer. I was told about this place, that it had lots of gold in a cave behind the house. I worked hard for a week digging and found nothing but hard rock and hard work. Somebody lied to me."

"How sad, Albert. Do you think this is the man who wanted you killed?"

"I would say it is, darling, and I agree it is very sad. I will do as he wished."

"The ground will be frozen below three inches. Put him in the place where he dug for the stupid gold and seal it with rock and clay. It will be a fitting place for him."

It took most of the next day to seal off the last ten feet of the tunnel, after placing Claude inside. A board with his name on it was all that was left as a reminder of him.

"I should not feel like this, but I hate losing the white buffalo more than the man we just buried, Albert. He was as harmless as a child. What do you think made him gore Claude?"

"Your guess is as good as mine, Molly. Could be he was trying to protect himself or maybe Claude would have killed one or both of us. That has been on my mind since we found him."

Molly suggested they wait for another week before planting any seed because the ground was still too cold. The farming tools were gone over and sharpened and several dead pines cut and hauled down to be sawed into blocks and split for firewood. At the end of the week, all the wood used during the winter was replaced with new wood. The days were getting longer and with the warm sunshine, everything began to green up.

"Don't plow too deep, Albert. Father said three inches is plenty, just enough to loosen the soil. The sun will warm the soil and the seed will sprout quickly if they are planted shallow."

The gang discs were no challenge for Big Tom to pull. At the end of the first day, the two-acre garden was turned over twice, and five days later, all the seeds were planted.

"Molly, let us pray God will bless this labor and give us a good harvest." After praying, Molly smiled and said, "This is the same kind of prayer my father always prayed. You remind me so much of him."

Albert was feeding the horses one morning when he looked across the valley and saw a half dozen buffalo feeding on the new tender grass. There were three baby calves and one of them was white. He ran back to the cabin yelling for Molly to come and see.

"What is so important, darling?"

He pointed to where the buffalo were. "There," he pointed.

She could hardly contain herself. They both walked as close as they dared so as not to scare them away. "Albert, this makes me so happy. Do you think Whitey is his father?"

"I would think so."

"I hope he will be as friendly as him. Something good was taken away and another good thing has taken its place. We are truly blessed, Albert."

All day, Molly was back and forth from the cabin to where the buffalo were. They got so used to her that she could get within a few feet of them. That evening, they had two visitors, Bogie and Singing Dove.

"We were sort of expecting Bogie," Molly exclaimed. "This is a wonderful surprise to have you come with him. Now I can share my home with my best friend as she did with me."

Albert and Bogie led the horses to the barn and the women went to the cabin.

"I have never been up here before, Molly. It is such a wonderful place and I can see why you never want to leave. White Wolf says it is not a good place up on the mountain in the wintertime for Indians. The old ones' spirits don't allow it."

"I am only one forth Indian, Singing Dove, but I don't believe in the old ones' spirits."

"I promised I would not stay long, just to make him happy. He thinks your mother would still be alive if she had not come up here."

"We never know why things happen, but I can assure you, God knows and his Word tells us it is all for the best. There is so much I want to show you and talk about and I still can't believe you are here."

When the men came in, Molly was preparing a meal. A pot of sage tea sat next to the fire. "It is not good English tea, Bogie, though I like it better than your bitter American coffee. Albert and I hardly ever drink coffee anymore."

When the meal was over, Bogie stood and started pacing. "There is something Dove and I want to talk to you two about." This was the first time Albert had ever seen him search for words.

"I tried to convince her it would not work. Now I want you to tell her. She will not listen to me. I am old enough to be her grandfather. It just will not work."

"You forgot to tell us what it is that won't work, Uncle Bogie," Molly said with a big smile she was trying to hide.

"Oh." He reached down and scratched his wooden leg as if it was itching. "She wants us to get married, her and me. This is the most absurd thing I have ever heard of. Tell her, will you?"

"Let your Dove tell us why she thinks it will work, Bogie." Albert answered. All but Bogie thought this humorous.

"I love this old man, as he calls himself, and he cannot deny he feels the same way towards me. He has never said so but I can tell. I feel when two people love each other, age does not matter. I have been asked by a lot of braves to be their wife. I never felt a thing for them. Bogie makes me feel all warm inside. Then, one day I knew why. I am in love with him."

"Okay," Molly said as she stood and motioned for Bogie to sit. "Singing Dove says she loves you, Bogie, even though you say you are too old to marry her. Is your age the only thing to stand in your way? If you tell her you don't want to marry because you don't love her, that would be reason enough. Can you truly say you do not love her?"

Bogie looked to melt in his chair. *I would be lying if I said I didn't love her*, he thought. *In ten years, I will be eighty and her thirty. That would be unjust to her.*

"Take all the time you need to answer, Bogie. This is a very important decision to make."

Again, Bogie thought about it and a smile began to form. "Aw heck. You win. I do love you, Dove, and I ask in front of these best friends of ours, will you marry this old man?"

"Yes, I will marry you," she said as tears appeared in her eyes. "Though I refuse to call you an old man. I will call you Bogie, the man I love."

"Well, I married you two, will you do the same for us?" Bogie asked Albert.

The Holy Bible was placed in front of Singing Dove and Bogie as the presence of God. The vows were made to each other and Albert and Molly were their witnesses.

The newlyweds were offered the cabin for the night, but refused. "We will take the tack room suite in the barn, just a pallet on the floor will do," Bogie answered.

This is the truth of how it all came about, the marriage of Bogie Anderson and Singing Dove.

"I am a happy married man," he announced. "I will now declare myself an Anderson, named after my real father, though he never claimed me as his own. If my wife and I have children, they will also be Andersons and heirs to the Anderson fortunes."

They did have a child, a robust healthy boy who they named after Albert's father, Phillip Anderson.

CHAPTER TEN

"This tack room could be made into a comfortable place with a little work, Dove," Bogie said the next morning. "How long do you want to stay here?"

"Forever, if I could. I have never seen a more beautiful place. It could be easy to envy our friends, though we promised White Wolf we would leave before winter set in."

"Then we will ask about making this room a little more comfortable. The two outside walls are sufficient and the two inside walls and ceiling will be easy to fix. A bed, a couple of chairs, a little table and some way to heat it and I say it will do."

Molly and Albert were sipping their tea when the newly-weds pounded on the door. Bogie wasted no time in asking if they could fix up the tack room for a place to stay for a little while.

"We could add an extension to this house if you are serious about staying," Molly answered.

"Your barn is plenty good. It will be perfect for us with a little work," Singing Dove said.

It was agreed upon and plans for the improvements would start.

"The planting is over and the grass for hay will not be ready for weeks. Now is the time for this to take place. I am so excited you will be here for a while, Singing Dove. Let the men take care of the improvements. We will make new clothes for all of us."

In three weeks, the building project was finished and hoeing the fast-growing grass from around the new seedlings became a priority until the plants grew enough to shade out the grass. Each day was spent working and after supper, they talked the evening away. Every day since Albert and Molly married, they spent a portion of their time reading and discussing the Bible. They invited Singing Dove and Bogie to join them in their devotionals.

"We were hoping we could join you," Singing Dove said. "Bogie and I often talk about how different you two are and decided it was what you learn from reading the Bible."

"It started when Grandfather asked me questions about what my plans were for the future. I didn't know at the time he was wondering if he could depend on me to help him with his vast holdings. I had no plans and said as much. It was not what he wanted to hear. When it finally did dawn on me what he wanted, I decided to take a serious look at myself and try and figure things out. That was when I first met you, Bogie. You planted a seed in my mind about America. I can look back now and see things fall into place, you taking time to train me in the art of survival, coming with me to this fine country, and us meeting up with White Wolf and his band. Then something occurred, I know now it was the Spirit of God that forced me to come up here where I met and fell in love with my sweet Molly. You cannot convince me these things just happened. I know without a doubt it was God. What he has for me in the future, I have no idea, but I want to be ready when he calls. Now, what about the both of you? Would you like for our God to be your God?"

Yes, was the immediate reply from the both of them.

"God's word tells us if we confess with our mouth the Lord Jesus, and believe in our heart that God raised him from the dead, you can be saved. For with the heart man believeth unto righteousness, and with the mouth confession is made unto salvation. Are you willing to accept this and ask him to come into your heart and be your Lord and Savior?"

Again, the answer was yes. "I don't understand all of this, Sonny, but I believe every bit of it. Is that enough?"

"If you believe and want this more than anything, it is enough. You now have the Holy Spirit of God in your heart to lead you and guide you in all things and it will definitely change your life. Praise the Lord."

The Bible study continued throughout the spring and summer. Bogie and Singing Dove grew in the Spirit and knowledge of God.

The vegetables were gathered in bushels. Some preserved in jars, though most were put in cold storage in the cellar under the house. Meat was preserved and food was plenty. All four cut the waist-high grass for winter hay. The barn loft was full and every vacant place in the barn packed. Stacks high as could be reached dotted the meadows.

"This should last till next year's crop comes in," Molly said. "All we need now is corn, oats and a few things we can't grow ourselves."

"We hate to go and leave you two up here by yourselves, but we promised to be down before it snows, and from the looks of things, the snow could come any time. Early the next day, Bogie and Singing Dove left the cabin, promising to come back in the spring. Molly and Albert decided to go to Denver and order grain for the horses and pick up what supplies they could carry back with them. The trip down takes two days hard ride and three to come back. They left before the sun was up, the horses full of energy and raring to go. Mid-day, two days later on Saturday, they entered the town of Denver. People crowded the streets. Albert had not seen this many people in one place for over a year. Just inside town, he noticed a church with boards nailed across the door and windows. He pointed it out to Molly. The mercantile store was two blocks from the church. They tied up at the hitch rail and made their way to the large counter. People were everywhere browsing, talking and some were buying.

"Afternoon, Miss Butcher. It is good to see you. I am sure sorry about your pa. Didn't know till it was all over and you had left town." A tall skinny man was talking.

"Thank you, Carl. It was kind of sudden. Do you still deliver supplies up on the mountain?"

"Yes ma'am," he said with a big smile. "What you need?"

"The usual amount of corn, oats, and a few other items."

Carl wrote the things Molly named off.

"Carl, I would like you to meet my husband, Albert Anderson."

Carl was momentarily caught off guard. *"This big man dressed in buckskin with a beard and long Indian braids just couldn't be married to little Moller Butcher."* Then he realized Anderson was offering his hand in friendship. "Glad to meet you, sir," Carl said as he shook hands with Albert.

"Tell me something, Carl. Why is the door to the church nailed up?"

"No preacher in town. Got himself run off and the town can't find anyone to take his place."

"Why?"

"Mr. Anderson, there are seven saloons in town and they say there is no room for any more. There was one church and the saloon owners said the town was not big enough for a church yet."

"What do the ones who used to go to church do?"

"We meet in different ones' houses and hold services. There are still a few of us around. We own the building, but none of us are comfortable preaching."

"What do you think would happen if a preacher came to town and opened the church doors? Would you come?"

"I don't know. Maybe, yes, I would come. Do you know of someone willing to try it?"

"I think I just might know someone. Can you get the word out that there will be services at the church tomorrow at ten o'clock in the morning?"

"Who and where is this person?"

"You will have to wait and see, but I will tell you this, he will not be easy to run off."

"Miss Molly, your order will start for your place the first

thing Monday morning. Now, I have a mission to tend to. See you in church tomorrow."

"Albert, you are not going to do what I think you are going to do, are you?"

"Darling, let's stable the horses and find a place to spend the night. We have a lot of praying to do."

The lamp never went out in the little boarding house room where Albert and Molly stayed Saturday night. The praying was silent but someone heard the prayers that were lifted up to heaven, and Carl spread the word.

Sunday morning, Molly cleaned their clothes as well as she could. They were wearing the new clothes she and Singing Dove made. Soft tanned leather made from bleached deerskin. Both had their hair in long braids Indian style and Albert trimmed his thick black beard. The hard and rigorous work Albert was accustomed to made his muscles bulge his clothes and one could see he would not be one to make mad. With his pistol in his wide belt and carrying his long rifle in one hand and a Bible in the other, he and Molly walked the few blocks to the church. When they arrived, there was already a crowd of people standing around, some curious, and some came to hear the new preacher. He handed Molly his rifle and Bible. "Hold this, would you please?" He kicked the bottom board and it splintered, so did the next one. The top board was torn away by the mere strength of his hands. There was a gasp from the crowd.

"What do you think you are doing?" someone across the street yelled.

Albert turned and walked to where the speaker was. "We are going to have church this morning, sir. Would you care to join us?" He grabbed the man by the hand and led him back to the church and up to the front row seats. "This will be your private pew from now on. What did you say your name was?"

The man mumbled, "Fred."

"Next Sunday, Fred, bring someone with you. We are going to fill this house and this town with God-fearing people. Now if all of you fine folks will just find a seat, it will take only a minute to open the windows. We want the ones passing to know the church in Denver is now, and in the future, open for praising the Lord."

While Albert was still speaking, he could hear the boards being torn from the windows. Light and fresh air began to flow through the building. He leaned his rifle against the podium and placed his pistol on top, next to his Bible. There was not a sound except a wagon going down the street.

He made eye contact with everyone there. He counted forty-four. "My name is Albert Anderson, and if you think I talk funny, it's because I do. I'm from England and they all talk this way. My beautiful wife, Molly, and I saw yesterday the doors on this house of God were closed. Can someone tell me why?"

After a moment, a little old lady spoke. "Because there are no men in this town, that's why."

"Ma'am, I see several men here this morning. You must be wrong."

"Not a one of them will stand against the saloon people," another lady spoke.

"I'm not here to disrupt this town. I am here to preach the Word of God. We will talk of this another time. I see you have a piano. Do we have someone to play it and to lead in a song or two?"

The church had been closed for over six months and the people were starved to have worship services again. The singing was loud and sweet and could be heard a long way off. Before the second song had finished, three large men walked in and stood just inside the door, each with a club in his hand. When the last stanza was finished, Albert asked the three men to be seated. Everyone turned to see who had come in and there was an instant fear from these men.

"You people sit quiet and do not do anything foolish. God and I will handle this," Albert said. "If you men want to hear the Gospel, have a seat. If it is trouble you want, we can supply that also. Which will it be?"

The largest of the three started up the aisle. "I'm going to teach you a lesson, preacher, and show these whimpering pups again what we do with preachers who come here." He was waving his club from side to side. Before anyone knew what happened, Albert shot the club out of the man's hand, ran, picked him up, and threw him into the other two with such force all three went flying into the street. He did not stop there. His big hard fist slammed against each of them. They were out cold when he piled them up in the middle of the street. The street had been deserted before the pistol shot, but was now crowded with onlookers, all wondering what was going on in the church. When Albert walked back into the church and began to preach, the house was full and others were looking through the windows.

Albert's first words, "I told you God was going to fill his house this morning. Now, let us see what else he has for us."

This was Albert's first sermon to preach in a church to a congregation. "Psalms 34:19, if you want to follow along. "*Many are the afflictions of the righteous, but the Lord delivereth him out of them all.* Throughout his Word, God talks about watching out for those who belong to him. This means he is watching out for you if you have placed your trust in him. He not only watches out for us, he protects us from all sorts of danger. His hand of protection delivers us from those who will do us harm. His all-seeing eyes, and his power to deliver us from evil forces, are two things we can count on."

The sermon lasted only a few minutes. The people sang a hymn and Albert dismissed the service in prayer.

A group of men asked if he could stay around a few minutes and talk with them.

Albert and Molly sat on the front bench and waited until they discussed something among themselves.

Carl, from the store, was the spokesman for the group.

"Brother Anderson, would it be possible to have you preach for us full time? First of all, we like the way you preach, and second, the way you handled those ruffians. We will back you one hundred percent."

"Thank you for your confidence. This is something my wife and I will have to pray about, and it will be I that will back you when you stand against this lawlessness here in Denver. I will let you know when I know. We will be leaving right away for home and will be waiting for you to deliver our supplies soon."

"They will be there in about three days if all goes well."

Nothing much was said about the church on their way back to the cabin. They knew there was much to pray about before serious talk began. Mid-day, three days later, they walked the tired horses into the barn.

"If you tend the horses, I will see we have a good hearty meal, Albert. I am about starved and I know you are also."

He gave them a rub down and a large helping of oats. He then forked generous amount of hay into their stalls. The door was left open so they could drink the cold fresh water from the creek.

"Okay boys, now it's my turn to fill my stomach."

"What are you going to do, Albert, about the offer?" Molly asked while they were eating.

"I don't know, darling. I have been thinking of nothing else. We will know when the time is right because God will show us. Do you have any suggestions?"

"I feel the same way. We will leave the matter up to the Lord. Let's clean the dishes then take a bath and go to bed early. I feel exhausted."

Albert slept sixteen hours, something almost unheard of. The smell of fried venison and the sound of Molly humming caused him to open his eyes.

"Morning, sleepy head," she said handing him a hot cup of sage tea.

That morning, Albert worked in the barn cleaning stables and other small jobs. He could not keep his mind on anything. "Lord, you know I want to do your will more than anything, but I have to know what your will is. Should I accept the church in Denver as pastor or not?"

The following day, Carl and his son, Robert, delivered the corn and oats. "Guess what happened?" were his first words. "Two of the saloons caught fire Sunday night and burned to the ground. One of them belonged to the Smith fellow who hired them roughnecks to teach you a lesson Mr. Anderson. That don't leave but five and two of them are talking about packing up before they lose everything they got. Let me tell you, all of Denver is talking about you and what you started."

Molly and Albert looked at each other and smiled. "Could this be our answer?" she asked.

Carl talked, while they unloaded the pack mules, about the men in the church making an about-face. "We have our town back and we like the feel of it. You thought any more about being our pastor?"

"Give me and Molly a few minutes and we will give you an answer. How much for the supplies?"

"The church didn't have time to pay you for preaching Sunday so they paid for this stuff."

"What do you think, Molly? Is this our answer?"

"I am thinking yes."

"Tell you what, we will go and have service with them Sunday and see what happens. I want to make sure we do the right thing."

"Sounds good to me," Carl said when Albert told him their decision. "We will be waiting then for your answer."

The next day, they left for Denver. They arrived on Saturday and stopped at the store to see Carl.

"Across the street is the best hotel in town, Mr. Anderson. A room is waiting for you and Miss Molly, free of charge as long as you want; another gift from the church members. My son will take care of your horses. Don't worry about them."

The room was large and comfortable. "We are being treated like special people, Albert. They must really like you."

"Looks to be the case, darling. I am looking forward to tomorrow. It's all up to the Lord."

Albert and Molly wanted to be the first at the church and so did about half the congregation. The building was sparkling clean from top to bottom, inside and out. Six more pews had been added since last Sunday.

"Want me to start ringing the bell?" one of the young boys asked Carl. Another asked if he could help. "Wait another ten minutes and take turns, not hard rings, easy and smooth. You are not going to believe this, Reverend, another saloon burned and two packed up and left town since I talked to you a few days ago," Carl added. "Only two left and they only open a while in the evenings."

"I hope you church people are not responsible for these burnings. It is not the way to deal with this sort of thing."

"Honestly, we don't know who is doing this."

The church filled to capacity with others standing and several outside. The song leader led in three congregational songs and Carl sang a beautiful special. Albert then went to the pulpit holding up his Bible. "I left my pistol at the hotel this morning, though I have a sword, the Word of God. This is the only weapon we will be using today. Before I get started, I want to say it would be disappointing if one of you were to be found guilty of burning these businesses out. There is a right way and a wrong way to do things. This is what we will be talking about today. Proverbs 16:25, *"There is a way that seemeth right unto a man, but the end thereof are the ways of death."*

"We all make choices in this life every day, some, we have cause to regret. Some, we are glad to have made them. Usually, the bad ones are the ones we don't pray about. We make them because it's right in our eyes. Just like burning the saloons, they thought it was the right thing to do at the time. I doubt seriously if they took time to pray about it. 'Vengeance is mine,' sayeth the Lord. If we let God handle these kinds of things, it will be done right in his eyes.

For some, it's okay to steal, kill, or whatever it takes to get what they want. This is a self-righteous person, which means he is right in his own eyes, but when he has to pay the consequences of his actions, he thinks it's too harsh. The law may never catch him, though one day he will stand before the Lord and give an account of all things. All of us will. Let us not look at things in our own eyes, but with the eyes of God."

Albert preached an hour this time before he gave the invitation to make things right with the Lord. It took most of another hour to end the service. The church committee asked Albert and Molly meet with them after all had left.

"Do you have an answer for us yet, Reverend?"

"We will try it on a trial bases, Carl. Molly and I have to talk some more and I would like to meet the people and know more of what would be expected of me.

If possible, let's have another service this evening."

"We were hoping for that. Everyone will get the message."

Time was set for five o'clock.

Albert and Molly talked about and decided to take the offer to pastor the church.

The evening crowd was not so large as the morning, though all the pews were full. When preaching was over, Albert made the announcement he would accept their offer to be their pastor until the Lord led him elsewhere.

Everyone seemed to be excited to have Albert and Molly and promised to help in any way they could. "The house next door belongs to the church, Reverend, but it needs some work to be a proper place to live," Carl said. "If you don't mind staying in the hotel for a while, we will start with the repairs tomorrow.

Another thing, will you be satisfied with seventy percent of what the church takes in for a salary plus the house? We took in fifty dollars today; your part would be thirty-five dollars."

"Good enough, Carl, and tell the committee thanks."

Two weeks later, the repairs were finished and they moved in. A brand new majestic wood stove with lots of shiny chrome was Molly's pride and joy. "I have never cooked on a stove before," she said. Some of the ladies promised to help her.

There were two bedrooms, a large kitchen and dining area combined, and a front and back porch. A barn and a large pasture with a spring fed creek were at their disposal. The horses had already been brought there a few days earlier and were glad to have a place large enough to run in.

"We are going to miss our mountain, Molly, darling, but I think this is where the Lord wants us to be, for now anyway."

"I am excited for this chance to try something different and to live around other people. This is all new to me. There is food in abundance up there and it should be brought down so we can use it before it spoils."

"I will mention this to Carl and see if we can use his mules. The grain and hay will be okay to leave there for a while until we see how this is going to work."

"Albert, I do hope this is what God wants us to do," she said with tears.

He hugged her. "Darling, I have felt from the very time I saw the church boarded up, this is where He wanted us and I still feel the same way. Now let's go fire up the stove and make us a hot cup of store-bought English tea.

CHAPTER ELEVEN

The church continued to grow in membership and in building size. A large addition was added on. Every day, Albert would visit, sometimes his members and sometimes those who did not go to church. He was a very good speaker and they all loved his English accent. He made himself known in the business community and the political arena. He was respected by all and had the same respect for everyone he met, rich or poor, young or old. Molly went with her husband whenever she could. She was a great asset to his ministry.

One Saturday, Albert and Molly visited a new family to their area. They had seven children, ages one year to ten years and all very mannerly. They promised to come to church the next day. On the way home, Albert could see Molly was in deep thought.

"You look to be a thousand miles away, darling. What's on your mind?"

"Do you think we will ever have children, Albert?"

"I am hoping we will," he replied with a smile. Those parents were raising their children the right way. Did you notice how respectful they were?"

"Yes, and the five-year-old girl with her white hair hanging in ringlets, I wanted to pick her up and hug her so much."

"This is something we will just have to ask God for, Molly. The Bible speaks of women doing that very thing and he answered their prayer."

The winter was mild compared to the ones on the mountain. Spring had come and most people were tilling their soil for their gardens, including Albert and Molly.

"Do you realize, Molly, we have been here seven months? It doesn't seem possible."

"I know, and I am so glad we are where we are. God has been so good to us. Living around friends makes me happy. I cannot ever see us or anyone living by themselves."

"Hey, Sonny! You are about as hard to find as a needle in a haystack."

They could not believe, Bogie and Singing Dove standing there with great big grins. She was expecting.

"Your note on the table said you were in Denver, but it didn't say where. It's a good thing everyone here knows you."

The greeting was touching. Molly could see Singing Dove was exhausted and wasted no time in getting her into the house where she could rest.

"Singing Dove, this is such a surprise to see you here and to see you are with child. How much longer before it's due?"

"A little over two months. We wanted it to be born on the mountain, but White Wolf insisted we return to the village for the birth."

"I am so sorry for all your troubles, Singing Dove. The thing to do now is to take care of you. Rest while I prepare a meal."

Later in the week, Singing Dove was rested and back on her feet. The journey from her village to the top of the mountain and back down to Denver had taken a lot out of her.

"White Wolf does not want the baby to be born on the mountain because he believes the spirits would not approve," Singing Dove said. "He says it will not be a healthy baby if it is born there. We told him you were born up there and you are healthy and strong."

Molly said they were welcome to live in the cabin if they wanted to go back up for the summer.

"No. I would like to stay here a few days. There is no climbing between here and our village. A week of easy going and we will be there. White Wolf will be happy."

"Molly and I will be here a year in September. I will ask for time off and we will come visit you and all our friends," Albert stated.

Molly did not want to see Singing Dove leave and offered to go with them so she could help with the baby until Albert could get off.

"No indeed. Your place is here with Albert. I will have more help than I need when the baby comes."

The spring and summer passed quickly. The church continued to push forward, having record numbers in attendance. The garden was bountiful also. Over half was given to those who were not able to raise a garden.

The Abbot family with the seven children did visit the church and after several times, joined. They were faithful members and Molly got to hold and hug little Sue, the one she thought so precious. This made her want her own child more and more. She and Albert prayed if it could be God's will they would have a child.

When the middle of September came, the church had a going away church picnic for Albert and Molly. "We already miss you, preacher. Hurry up and get back here," was repeated over and over by the congregation. We should be back in three weeks or less was the reply. Three days was the estimated time for traveling. The first day, the wind blew cold off the mountain from the west, and at times, little flurries of snow spitted at them. The second day, the sunshine was almost too hot and the coats came off. Early the third day, Molly was getting anxious. "Albert, I can hardly wait to get there. What do you think Singing Dove has, a girl or boy?"

"Big as she was, maybe one of each. In a few hours, we will know."

When they stopped at noon to rest the horses and eat, Albert said he had been here once on one of their hunting trips. "It won't be long now, darling."

When they were a mile from the village, a half dozen horses came at a dead run towards them around a bend in the trail. Their eyes had a wild look and they paid no attention to the two riders.

"Something is bad wrong, Molly." He slipped his long rifle from its boot and Molly did the same. "Let's go, but be careful." Dap also knew something was wrong. He took off at a fast run with Big Red close behind. Two shots were fired as they rounded the bend. *Bogie*, he thought, has the only guns in the village.

There were Indians on horses and others on the ground shooting arrows, throwing spears and hatchets. It looked like the whole Comanche nation was there. Two more shots rang out. Where did they come from? A Comanche wearing a war bonnet came at him holding a spear. Albert shot him, then he shot two more with his double-barreled pistol his grandfather had given him. Two more shots from Bogie and the Comanche turned to leave. Dap reared when a wounded Indian slashed at him with a knife.

Albert fell and landed on his feet. Bogie appeared next to him, then yelled and shoved him. The first thing Albert saw was Bogie with a spear through him, with his silly smile, looking at him.

"Well, Sonny, you made it, and just in time I'd say."

"Why did you do that? Oh, Bogie."

"Look over in my teepee, Sonny, and you will know why," Bogie said in a soft whisper. "Bury us together in the same hole and raise little Phillip like you would raise your own. Dove and I would appreciate it. My little Dove and me are going to be with our Lord and we thank you and Molly for showing us the way. See you on the other side, Sonny."

The tears flowed as Albert rocked back and forth holding Bogie. For how long, he did not know. Boy, with part of his wooden leg missing, sat beside them and said not a word. People crying was what made him look around.

Then he remembered and ran to the teepee. Molly was there holding a baby. Her best friend, Singing Dove half covered with a blanket. "They scalped her, Albert. They took her beautiful hair," screamed Molly. "Why would they do such a thing?"

Darkness fell on a group of weeping Ute Indians. Of the forty-six, twenty survived, and some of them were severely wounded. White Wolf was one of the casualties. All night, eerie sounds of the mourning and crying could be heard. Albert and Boy dug a grave large enough for Bogie and Singing Dove and lay them side by side as Bogie had asked. Molly, holding baby Phillip, watched and prayed. Stones were placed over the mound. Albert made a cross and placed it at the head of the grave.

"Why would they do such a thing?" Molly asked again.

"Our horses," Boy said. "They wanted our beautiful spotted horses. First, Raven came and told us there was a herd of buffalo five miles away. He thought all of the able men of the village would go on a hunt. He is an evil man. My father was suspicious and only sent Runner and Red Fox to see. A few minutes later, the Comanche came. If it were not for you and Bogie, they would have killed us all. One day I will make him pay for this. You will see."

"No, Boy. I will make him pay. He is a liar and deceiver," Runner said with anger. He and Red Fox heard the rifle fire three miles away. By the time they returned to the village, the Comanche were gone with most of the horses.

Albert and Molly stayed several days to help care for the injured.

"There is a small army fort near Denver if your people are able to travel. We can all go together and you can set up your camp near there. This is not a good place for you now. The Comanche may come back," Albert informed the village a few days after the attack. Albert gave Bogie's rifle to Runner, and his pistol, he gave to Boy. "He would like you to have them." Bogie had taught both how to use and care for the weapons.

Runner was the one who seemed to be in charge now. He talked with the others about going to live by the army fort and all thought it a good idea. There were ten horses including Dap and Big Tom. The rest were taken in the massacre.

The evening before they were to depart, Molly suggested to

Albert that it may be a good idea for him to go ahead of them back to Denver and get others with wagons to help transport the older and crippled. "The rest of us can go at a slower pace. There is not enough food to last for the distance we have to travel," she said.

Albert left two hours before daylight calculating he could make it to Denver in two days. The Indians left a while later with the ones who could not walk, riding horseback or on a travois, while the others took turns walking and riding. The journey was slow, making twelve miles a day.

Baby Phillip was just two months old and needed milk. One of the mares had a colt and had to share his milk with Phillip. At first, he refused to drink it which caused much anxiety for Molly. One of the older women suggested she sweeten it slightly with honey which was in abundance. After a few tries, he finally decided to drink it.

Albert rode into Denver late the second day on a very tired Dap. The first place he went was to see Carl. He explained the situation and asked if he would get several people from the church with wagons to help transport the small band of Indians to the fort.

"We'll be ready when you are, reverend. Just give us a time."

After settling on a time, Albert bathed, fell across his bed and was instantly asleep. There were eight men with wagons and extra horses waiting for him the next morning.

"I thank each of you for your concern. These people are in desperate need of your help."

It took two and a half days to reach the Indians. They had not gone as far as was expected. One of the most seriously wounded could not go any further so they stopped for him to get his strength back.

Carl brought what medicine he thought may be needed to treat them. Several large pots of food were prepared and all ate their fill.

Immediately when arriving, Albert went to where Molly

was feeding Phillip. He hugged them both. "Molly, darling, how are you and Phillip doing? I could not wait to get back here again. Let me hold him while you rest. I know you must be worn out."

"I have to admit I am. These poor people could not go any further. I am so glad we have all this help."

They decided to stay where they were for another day. The Indians and their ponies were exhausted. The teepees, along with their belongings, had been hauled this far on them.

When they left, five of the wagons were loaded with all the belongings and supplies. The other three carried the feeblest of the Indians. Everyone else had a horse. The third day, they parked the wagons outside the fort. The stockade was like most, pointed poles placed in the ground in an acre square with only one entrance. A fast running creek, fifty yards away.

Albert, Carl, Runner, and Boy, whose wooden leg had not yet been mended, were given permission to enter the compound. They were brought to the commanding officer's office. They introduced themselves and asked if the twenty Indians could set up their dwellings close by the fort.

"Absolutely not," the captain in charge stood and addressed Albert. "Reverend, with all respect for you, I will not tolerate any Indian to pitch his tent within ten miles of here. I am stationed out here in this forsaken wilderness to subdue these savages. They cannot be trusted and I will not allow it."

"Captain," Albert said, these are Ute Indians and they have never committed one hostile act against any white man. They have in times past, sided with our military against other Indians and have served as scouts and interpreters for years. I can see you cannot tell one tribe from another."

"Sir, an Indian is an Indian, and I say again, none will be allowed to live near here."

Top Sergeant Murphy was standing next to the door and asked permission to speak. "Yes, sergeant, what is it?"

"Captain Foxley, I know these Indians. Their Chief is White Wolf, a good friend of mine, and I have spent lots of time with them through the years. This man here is Runner, the best there is at scouting and tracking."

Runner spoke, "Thank you, sergeant, for what you say. White Wolf no longer lives. The Comanche has killed him, along with over half my people. They came to steal our horses and they will be looking for trouble with the white soldiers. You had better be on guard from now on." Then he addressed the captain. "I know most of your men here, Foxley. They are my friends. If they were not, I would not tell you this. You and your men are in grave danger. The Comanche have over one hundred fighting braves; you have only forty-two men here. True, you have guns and they don't, not now anyway. They will starve you out. Get all the water you can. They will be coming."

Captain Foxley had never fought Indians before nor was he ever in a battle of any kind. This talk about one hundred fighting Indians attacking his little fort began to scare him.

"How many of your people are out there?" the captain asked.

"We are twenty in all, Foxley, but if you feel you cannot trust us, we will find another place."

"If Sergeant Murphy trusts you and you promise to help if we are attacked, set up where ever you want."

"We will do what we can, though it won't be much. There are only nine men able to fight."

Albert and the men of the church spent two more days helping with the teepees. They had brought several of the better ones which were not too damaged in the battle with the Comanche.

"Runner, do you believe the Comanche are going to try to attack this fort?" Albert asked.

"Yes, and soon I would say. They need guns and where best to get them? I have heard it talked about my friend."

"If this is the case why don't you and your people come to Denver with us. They would never try to overpower a town so big."

"My people will not go where there are so many whites and

I will not ask them to, but I thank you my friend."

Albert asked Boy if he would like to travel with them to Denver. One of his friends knew how to repair his damaged leg. There were only approximately twelve miles from the fort to Denver. Boy was excited. Never had he been this far from his own village. Molly and Phillip rode in one of the wagons with Albert riding beside them. In two hours, they reached their destination. Boy could not believe there could be so many people in one place.

"Where did all these people come from?" he asked excitedly. "Bogie told me about the big cities with lots of people but I did not understand it to be like this." He wondered about the many buildings and why the houses had to be so large. Even the doors amazed him and the windows could be raised to let in the cool breeze. He walked through the house in wonder at the many things he had never seen before.

Molly was exhausted when they got home. She fed Phillip with real cow's milk, which he did not like, and tucked him in bed with her. Albert and Boy went to see if they could get his leg fixed. About two inches of the bottom was broken off which made him walk with a limp.

"No problem," the blacksmith said. "You want it repaired with hard wood or something a little fancier like brass?"

He showed them a two-inch round bar of the brass. "Shines up real nice and should never break. For a big boy like you, a friend of our pastor, it won't cost a dime."

They settled on the metal. The smithy wanted Boy to stay while he measured and fitted the brass to the wood. Boy related to him about the massacre and their move to the fort.

Albert went and talked to Carl about more supplies for the little band of Indians. They decided to wait until Sunday and let the church help.

"Look at my new leg, Molly. See how it shines? He put new leather straps on it, too!" Molly was walking in the yard when Boy came running towards the house. He did a somersault and then a flip.

"Wonderful, Boy. It all looks new."

"That's because he sanded the wood and completely redone the whole leg. I can't wait to show everyone at the village."

After he spoke, big tears came into his eyes. "Why did they kill my father and my best friend, Bogie?" Molly held him close while he cried.

"We will never know why some people do these things. I know how you must feel losing your father and friends. In time, there will be new friends and the hurt will get less so don't let your anger destroy you like it does so many people. Albert and I are here for you anytime."

"I know you are, Molly, and if I can, I would like to stay here for a while. There is so much I don't know. Bogie taught me a lot of things about the white man's way of doing things, but I didn't know there were so many white people. He was teaching me how to read and write, but now he is gone."

"We will talk to Albert when he gets back. I am sure he will be glad for you to stay with us."

Albert was glad Boy wanted to stay in Denver with them and desired an education.

CHAPTER TWELVE

"Absolutely not," Mr. Hibbit, the school principal, said when Albert brought Boy to school a few days later. "There will be no Indians in any school of mine. Everyone knows you cannot teach them how to read or write. It is just not in them to be able to understand our ways. They cannot be trusted in any way to do what is right."

This outburst was completely unexpected by Albert. He left the school without saying a word. The three-man school board committee agreed with Mr. Hibbit. "The people in this town would be in an uproar if we let an Indian in our school."

Molly was infuriated when they came home and explained what had happened. "Can they do this in a public school?" she asked.

"They seem to be able to do what they want, darling. I talked to Carl and he said it took two years to get a qualified teacher out here and Mr. Hibbit agreed to teach only if he were given complete authority. I agree with you. It is not right but this is the way it is." Albert took Molly's hands in his. "We have a bigger problem than the school. Carl also said if we brought Boy to church, most of the people will quit coming."

Molly could not believe what she had just heard. "Why would they do such a thing, Albert? Can they love God and hate a little boy who never harmed anyone? Are you saying this child cannot go to church with us?"

"I will go back to my village. I understand all white people are not like you and all Indians are not like me. Bogie told me about his God and I want to know more about him. I believe he loves Indians as much as he loves anyone."

"That he does, Boy. God looks at the heart, not the color. You are just as precious to him as anyone else and never forget it," Molly exclaimed.

After Boy was asleep, Molly asked Albert what were they going to do about the situation?

"For now, we pray for God's direction. He will show us his divine will in this. Sunday is in two days; the church can help in this matter."

"Albert, there is something else on my mind. Do you think us praying for a child was wrong? We now have a baby, but I didn't want one the way it came about. For some reason, I feel Bogie and Singing Dove's death may have been our fault for praying the prayer we prayed."

"Darling, don't even think like that. God works in mysterious ways and I believe we were sent there at exactly the right time. Ten minutes later, and the whole village would have been slaughtered, even little Phillip. Don't ever feel guilty. God doesn't make mistakes."

When Sunday arrived, Albert, Molly, Boy and little Phillip dressed in their finest clothes. Molly had cut Albert and Boy's braids off where they looked like the other men. Boy was dressed in regular clothes, which he did not like, though he agreed to wear them. He had the new brass part of his wooden leg polished to a high shine.

They were the last to arrive and everyone watched them walk in and take their places. Carl started the services with singing as usual. Albert knew immediately some in the congregation were upset. When he took his place behind the podium, Molly thought he was the most handsome man she had ever seen.

His hair and beard trimmed, wearing a new white shirt made him look different she thought, or was there something else; he looked completely at ease and sure of himself. Then she knew, he had received his answer from God. The church would have a choice to make. His sermon was taken from Joshua 24:15,

"Choose this day whom ye will serve, as for me and my house, we will serve the Lord."

"We make choices every day. Sometimes we make bad ones and have to deal with the consequences. Then there are times we make good ones and things work out fine. What works best for me is prayer. I try and seek God's divine will in all decisions and choices I have to make. My wife and I are facing one now, so are you." He asked Boy to come stand by him. "We have been told this child is not welcome to come to this church and worship with us. If this be the case, my wife and I cannot worship here either. This is the choice you have to make and I plead with you to make it a matter of prayer. We will have the congregation vote in the evening service, and we will abide with the majority vote."

Albert and his small family left so the church could discuss the matter without their presence.

"What do you think will happen, Albert, when the vote is taken? Are you serious about resigning?"

"Yes, darling. Christ died for all and if children are banned from worship, we are wasting our time here."

They had just finished the noon meal when Carl and two more deacons knocked on the door.

"We have already taken our vote, Reverend," he said smiling. "Sixty-five to two in your favor. Now let me tell you the good part. We also talked to Mr. Hibbit and the school board. They can be replaced easier than you and we told them so. Boy can start classes in the morning."

The evening service consisted of a sort of picnic with the church members welcoming Albert and his family saying how glad they were to have them stay.

"I hope Boy doesn't have problems at school," Molly said when they were walking home after church. "I wish you would go with him in the morning."

Boy was a little nervous and also excited when he and Albert entered the two-room schoolhouse. Mr. Hibbit met them at the door and told Boy to go inside and find a desk.

"I don't know how you turned this town against me, preacher, and I want to tell you what I told them. Indians are not capable of learning like whites and I will not give him extra privileges. If he cannot cut it, he will have to go."

"Now let me tell you, teacher, this Indian is as smart as anyone else and if given the same opportunity as the others, he will be at the top of his class in no time and this is a promise. While I am here, I would like to invite you to our church service next Sunday. It would be good for us to get to know each other better."

Without another word, Mr. Hibbit went inside and slammed the door.

"Lord, please watch over Boy and change Mr. Hibbit's way of thinking about him."

Boy came home after school bubbling over with excitement talking about his new friends. "Everyone wanted to feel my wooden leg and hear about how I got it, even some of the girls. They said I don't look like other Indians. I told them my father was a chief and half white."

"Did you have to read or write something for the teacher?" Molly asked.

"I did both. Mr. Hibbit put me in the third grade. He said I was smarter than I look. He is a grouch, but I kind of like him. Some of the kids wanted to know if I could run and play ball. I told them I could run a little, but I have never played their kind of ball. I didn't want them to think I was a show off."

"We are so happy for you, Boy. Albert and I want you to have an education like other children."

"Did Bogie teach you to read and write?" Albert wanted to know.

"My Father, White Wolf, taught me first. His father was a teacher and taught him and anyone who wanted to learn. Many of our tribe learned to speak some English though not many wanted to learn more than that. Bogie not only made it possible for me to run and walk again, but also taught me to think for myself. Also, we talked of his God and the things he learned from you."

"Bogie was a wonderful person, Boy. He is the reason I came to America. He also taught me many things. We both lost a great friend and Bogie would be proud of you. Do your best in school and things will work out. An education will open up a whole new world for you."

That evening, Boy wanted to talk to Albert and Molly about his name. "The ones in my class say Boy is not a real name. They don't think of names like Indians do. I tried to explain my name would change when I get older. Do you think this is a good time to change my name?"

Molly agreed this would be as good a time as any and asked if he had a name picked out.

"Bogie was my best friend and I believe it would be wrong to take his name. Bo is close if you think it will be alright."

"I think it would please him," Molly said.

"Could I also use Anderson for a last name?"

"It will please me," Albert said. "Bo Anderson, it is."

"It is a good name," Boy said with a big smile. "I can't wait to tell them at school."

Bo Anderson soon won the admiration of most all the students in his school, even the teacher, Mr. Hibbit. They all liked Bo telling of his life living as an Indian, about how he lost his leg and of Albert and Bogie coming to their village one day.

Bo said he thought he would always be a cripple until he saw Bogie had a wooden leg and could run as fast as their fastest runner and do anything he wanted to.

"I bet I could out run him if he was still around," sixteen-year-old Jake said. I have never been beat yet and a lot of people have tried."

"You are fast, Jake. I've watched you play ball, but you would not have been a match for Bogie. I think I can run as fast as you," Bo continued.

"You little squirt, I knew you were a blowhard. I can walk faster than you can run."

"Alright boys, let us get back to our studies," Mr. Hibbit

said. "There will be no racing during school hours."

Bo knew sooner or later he would have to prove himself. Jake felt challenged and had no intention of letting this go.

Bo went straight to Molly after school. "I didn't mean to say what I said about me running faster."

"Can you out run him?" Molly asked.

"I'm not sure. I think I can, but I haven't run for a long time."

"Tell you what," Albert said, "I haven't run in a long time either. It would do us both good to get some exercise."

Three days a week they rode their horses to the outskirts of Denver and ran for two hours. At first, Bo lagged behind, but little by little his speed picked up until he could keep the same pace as Albert.

"I'm still not fast as Bogie, but I think I can outrun Jake," Bo said after a month of training.

Jake asked Bo every few days if he was ready for a race and he would answer, "Not now." After the first month of training, Bo said he was ready but the race had to be outside of town with no one around.

"You scared, little squirt? You challenged me in front of people, now you have to take your medicine."

"If I have too, I will," Bo agreed, "but first come with me to my house. I want to show you something."

Jake agreed to follow Bo if he would race him where the school could watch.

Just the two boys walked behind the barn where Bo lived.

"What did you want to show me, squirt?"

"Watch." He took off like a bullet, ran the three hundred yards to the back fence, turned, and with faster speed, came back to where Jake was standing. Twenty feet before stopping, he went high into the air, executed a flip and landed in front of Jake who was unable to say a word.

"Jake, you are too good a friend to show you up in front of the kids at school, but if you insist we can have the race."

"Where did you learn to run so fast, Bo? I have never seen

anyone so fast."

"Like I said the other day, my best friend Bogie taught me, and he was faster than me, much faster."

Jake never mentioned racing again and, from then on, he believed every word Bo said.

The first year of school passed quickly. Bo was at the top of his class and far exceeded expectations. Mr. Hibbit was the first to admit he was wrong about Indians not being able to learn like anyone else. "Bo will go far, reverend," He told Albert and Molly. "He should be in at least the sixth grade, and if you don't object, we will place him there next year."

"If you are sure, it will be fine with us," Albert said.

After school was out for the year, Albert asked the church for a few days off so he could bring Bo to visit with his people.

Bo was excited and could not wait to see his friends again. "Do you think they will remember me he asked? It has been almost a year."

"They will remember," Molly answered, smiling at his excitement.

"Will they remember little Phillip?" he asked again, holding the baby's hands while coaxing him to walk.

"He has grown a lot, but they will remember him also."

Runner was the first to see them coming when they neared the fort. By the time they entered the small village, everyone was outside to greet them. The few children converged on Bo and he excitedly told them of his life in the big city of Denver.

The men took Albert to White Wolf's teepee to talk while Molly joined the women. They could not believe how much Phillip had grown; he was beginning to walk with help. A feast was prepared in honor of their visit.

Albert wanted to know if there had been any trouble from the Comanche or the solders at the fort.

"We haven't heard from the Comanche and we go inside the fort only if we need something," Runner exclaimed. "They don't bother us and we stay away from them. There has been no trouble."

Chief White Wolf's teepee had been erected just as if he were still alive. Runner insisted they stay there as long as they were at the village.

As evening approached they gathered to eat. Runner stood and gave a welcome speech. "We want to thank you," he pointed to Albert and Molly. "If it were not for you, we would all be dead. You taught us many things and know how we used to live. At one time, we were many people, now we are a few. A proud people, now what you see are a dependent people. Our chief is dead along with many more and we have nothing to look forward to. Our beautiful spotted ponies we use to have were stolen by our enemies we thought to be our friends. We have not forgotten and we never will."

What Runner said broke Albert's heart. No longer was he a carefree and happy person, not the man he once was. Anger and a hunger for vengeance completely consumed him.

Molly also saw what he had turned into and that night when her, Albert and Phillip went to their teepee, she mentioned it.

"Runner blames himself for what happened, darling. He was not there when the Comanche came to the village. They tricked him into going to look for a heard of buffalo."

"Can he ever get over this, Albert?"

"Only with the Lord's help. I will try and reason with him when we are by ourselves."

Bo spent the night with a friend his age and stayed awake most of the night sharing the happenings since they last saw each other.

"Come go with me, Runner. I want to talk to Captain Foxley," Albert said the next morning. The two guards opened the gate as they approached.

The captain saw them enter the compound and motioned them in to his office. "Glad to see you again, preacher. I heard you were at the village."

"We come to visit our friends for a few days, captain, and wanted to check with you while we are here. I know tomorrow is not Sunday, but with your permission, I would like to have a preaching service here at the fort."

"Permission granted, reverend. We don't have a chaplain and the men would like to have church. We will be assembled at ten o'clock in the morning. You and your wife are welcome to stay inside the fort as long as you are here."

"We are fine staying in the village, captain, but I thank you for the offer."

Upon leaving the fort, Albert told Runner he wanted to talk to him away from the village. They stopped by the creek and Albert asked him to talk about why was he so angry.

"You are not angry they killed your best friend and his wife without a cause?" Runner asked.

"In a way, I am, though hurt is a better word. I understand how you feel, Runner, and what they did was awful. Any time someone takes a life, it is awful, and the hurt will always be there. There is a difference in being angry and being hurt. Anger is an emotion which will destroy a person. My God says vengeance belongs to him. He will take care of it."

"I will kill Raven myself and I don't need help from any God. The time will come and I will find him, and I have been thinking on ways to make him suffer."

"Once, you wanted to know more about my God. Do you still want to know?"

"Where was your and Bogie's God when he was needed? Tell me this, Albert."

"You will never understand the answer to such a question, Runner, as long as you have revenge in your heart. It is time we go back to the village. Think on what we have talked about."

Albert related his discussion with Runner to Molly. "There looks to be no way to reach him now and if he continues his obsession on getting revenge, he will destroy himself completely."

The next morning, Albert preached a great sermon to the soldiers and most of the Indians. Runner was not there.

"What an inspiring message, reverend," Captain Foxley said after the service. He then asked if Albert would meet with him for a few minutes.

"I was going to talk to you yesterday, but I didn't want to in front of your friend, Runner. I guess you noticed we have a few more men than when you were last here, ten more to be exact. Also, the army has sent me a shipment of much better rifles. This is guarded information, reverend. Again, I refer to Runner. He says we should wage a surprise attack on the Comanche before they attack us. What do you think about this?"

"Captain, one never knows what the Indians will do. Personally, I would advise against such action. As far as I know, the Comanche are peaceful at this time and Runner has personal reasons for wanting you to do this. Don't play his game."

"That is what Sergeant Murphy said. I just wanted to get another opinion. Thank you again, reverend, for preaching to us today. You are welcome to share the Word with us anytime."

"I don't have time to ride out to the Comanche village now, Molly. We have to be back in Denver in a couple of days, though soon I have to make the trip. Runner is trying to get the military involved in his evil doings."

Albert looked for Runner before leaving but to no avail. One of the men said he saw him leave camp that morning, but no one had seen him since.

Bo talked all the way back to Denver, excitedly telling of the things he and his friend had done. "I tried to get them to play games, but they said no one was allowed to laugh and play inside the village. We must respect the dead, Runner told us."

****

"Let me carry Phillip," Albert volunteered, walking home after the morning service. "I know you must be tired holding him all the time."

"He does get heavy after a while but I love taking care of him. It breaks my heart when I think of Singing Dove and Bogie not seeing him grow up. Albert, I miss them something awful."

Albert placed his arm around her as they walked the rest of the way home. "I think about them most every day, darling. We will make sure Phillip knows the kind of people his parents were. Uncle Bogie said to raise him as we would raise our own, and this we will do, but he must know his real parents."

Before evening service, Carl and his sixteen-year-old son, Robert, stopped by to talk to Albert. "He won't settle for anything but talking to you, pastor. He told me something and I said what's done is done, but he has to talk to you."

"Let's go inside and you tell me what it is bothering you, Robert."

"I just told Papa part of it, Pastor Anderson. There are more things I need your opinion on."

"Well, Son, let's hear it all," Carl said irritated.

"It was I, sir, who burned the first saloon, but not the rest. I heard the owner tell those three men to work you over and run you out of town like they done the last preacher. Honest, I had nothing to do with burning the others. I made sure no one was in there before I burned it."

Both Carl and Robert stared at Albert to see what he would say and do.

"Let's see, it has been over a year ago. There is no one here to bring charges against you in a legal matter. The only other thing is to get it right with God. Have you confessed this to the Lord and asked him to forgive you?"

"Many times, sir."

"I am sure he has forgiven you, Robert. As Christ would say, go and sin no more. Now what is the other thing you need help on?"

"I want to preach. I want to be a preacher like you. I feel this is what I have to do."

Carl just stared at his son before he spoke. "I thought you wanted to work in the store, Son. That is what you have said since you were a little boy."

"I know, Papa, but the Lord has been dealing with me for

quite a while, and it is all I can think about."

"I suggest you give it time, Robert. Put it off as long as you can. Wait for a few weeks and we will talk about it again."

Both Carl and Robert left feeling somewhat better, though Albert wondered if he had done the right thing. He remembered when the Lord was dealing with him and if God is calling Robert to preach his word, he must give him encouragement.

Molly agreed this would be number one on their prayer list, to pray for Robert.

Albert could not get Runner off his mind. He knew in his condition if he were not able to get the military to fight his battle, he would try and persuade the Comanche to attack the fort. Either way, a lot of the Comanche would be slaughtered and this was what he wanted. He felt he must try and stop it from happening.

"Molly, I have to go talk to the Comanche before Runner does something stupid. Will you be alright staying by yourself for a few days?"

"I will be fine, though I worry about you. What if they take you for an enemy? They can be so cruel, Albert."

"This is something we will put in God's hands, darling. After church tomorrow, I will ride out to the fort and talk to Captain Foxley."

Albert went directly to the fort instead of to the village. All the guards knew him by this time and quickly opened the gate when they saw him approach.

"I am here to talk to your captain, sergeant. Is he in?"

"Yes sir, reverend, in his office."

Foxley was sitting on his small porch enjoying the cool evening breeze.

"Good to see you again, reverend, business or pleasure?"

"I am hoping to find out about Runner and the Comanche. Have you seen either one?"

The Captain said Runner was in a few hours ago saying it would not be long before the fort would be under attack.

"That Indian is trying to make trouble, preacher. I am

thinking about placing him under arrest."

"Let me talk to him before you do."

Albert explained he was here to go talk to the Comanche chief. That would be a good place to start.

"If I'm not back in a week, come and look for me, captain."

He then went to the village just outside the fort where he found Runner and others waiting for him. They saw when he rode in and was wondering if something was wrong.

"No, Runner, I am going to talk to the Comanche and thought you would like to come along."

"I don't talk to them dogs," he said angrily. "You want to get the rest of us killed?"

"If you are afraid, I will go by myself."

This really made Runner angry. "Afraid of them old women, never. I will go with you and spit in their face."

"I go as a friend, and if you come with me it will be as a friend also. We don't know exactly who was involved when your village was attacked so, until we do, there will be no accusations."

"There were Comanche everywhere, Albert, and you know, you saw them."

"I saw Indians, Runner. You were not even there, and this is what angers you so. Now, talking is what we do, nothing else. Not until we have the facts."

"We will leave in the morning and you will get your facts, Albert Anderson."

CHAPTER THIRTEEN

It was still dark when the two riders left the next morning. As usual, Dap was ready to move at a rapid pace. Runner's spotted pony was just as eager. A mid-summer cool breeze blew off the mountains.

"It will take two days to get to Red Cloud's village," Runner said, "unless you want to take the short way over the Old Ones' burying place."

"Is it supposed to be sacred? If so, we will stay away from there."

"Don't tell me you are afraid of the Old Ones."

"Not afraid, Runner, just respectful."

After two hours of the fast pace, the horses were ready to slow. The sun began to warm the air as the time neared midday. They hardly spoke all morning.

A shallow stream crossed the trail and both horses stopped to drink the cool water. Albert dismounted and loosed his saddle and told Runner to let the horses graze for a while.

"What kind of man is Red Cloud?

"He is Comanche, that should tell you."

"This tells me nothing, only that he is an Indian. When he rode with us to find Molly and Boy the time Raven kidnapped them, he seemed fine to me. He even wanted to take Raven's life."

"You should not have stopped him. My people would be alive if you had not."

"Maybe you are right if one was to look at it in such a way, but no harm was done to Molly or Boy. He had changed his mind and was bringing them back to us."

"You think like a white man. I am Indian and think like an Indian. We are different."

Albert did not want to push the issue so made no more comments.

A little before dark, they stopped and kindled a small fire behind several large boulders next to the side of a cliff. Runner hobbled his horse and Albert turned Dap loose for the night. Again, there was very little conversation between them. They shared venison jerky and water from a canteen before wrapping in their blankets.

When it was light enough to see, they moved out. Again, the horses were rested and ready to go. Albert was thinking of how he would approach Red Cloud with their problem. *What if he deliberately led the surprise attack against White Wolf and his people? Would he take vengeance against him and Runner? He didn't seem like such a person, though I just met him one time.*

He was thinking on these things when Runner said something. The terrain had changed and they were now in a vast prairie where one could see for miles.

On their right and left were small groups of Indians. Runner said, "They are behind us also, Comanche."

"How much further to their village?" Albert asked.

"Three hours at most."

They kept their same pace and the Comanche did not try and stop them. By the time the village came into view, many more were following.

Albert had never witnessed such a sight. It looked as if the teepees stretched for a mile. They rode straight through the middle of them, dogs barking and people standing outside. Midway the village, the Indians who were following, surrounded them and two took the reins of their horses and led them to a huge teepee.

"Red Cloud was standing outside the entrance in his finest clothes and a headdress with eagle feathers which touched the ground behind him. The ones who brought them in said something to him and he answered. The two men holding their horses motioned them to dismount. Red Cloud entered his dwelling and Albert and Runner followed. Three more men sat side by side on the robes that covered the floor. They also dressed in beautifully-made leather clothes.

"These are his sub chiefs," Runner spoke quietly.

The chief sat next to the other three men, so Albert and Runner sat facing them.

Albert did not understand when the chief spoke. "He asked what were we looking for in his village," Runner interpreted.

"If you do not understand, I will speak your English. Did you lose your wife again, Albert Anderson?" he asked smiling.

"No not this time. We come for answers, Chief Red Cloud. I am surprised you remember me."

"You are the one who lives on the mountain with the spirits of the Old Ones. It is good to see you again."

"My wife and I now live in the place they call Denver. I tell the people about the God I serve, they call it church."

"Did you come here to talk about your God?"

"Not this time unless you want to hear about him."

"I know what you want but ask anyway. Then we will eat and talk of other things. Your friend here has a troubled spirit, does he not? He will be told the truth before the day is over, then he may have peace."

Runner could not wait to ask why he and his warriors attacked and killed so many of the Ute people.

The three sub chiefs' countenance changed to anger and Red Cloud motioned them to wait.

"Who did you see attack your people?"

Runner stood and started to say something and Albert pulled him back down. "Just answer the question, Runner."

"You know I was not there, but the attackers who were killed were Comanche."

No one spoke for what seemed a long time until Red Cloud broke the silence.

"How many of the ones killed were Comanche?"

"I counted three."

"How many killed were not Comanche?"

"Fifteen others were killed, they were all together."

"What else did they do besides kill your people?"

"They stole our spotted horses, the ones you get from us."

"Because you don't know, I will tell you. I could kill you for accusing us of something we did not do; this is what these other chiefs want. If I were you, I would feel the same as you, maybe. Raven and six more of our people that he persuaded to join him, and I don't know how many Cheyenne, attacked your people. He wants to make a name for himself is what I think. When we heard of his attack on your people, twenty of our men followed them to bring them back. When they crossed the mountains to the west, our men came home, all except one, the father of a young Comanche boy who joined Raven's band. He was shot and will never be right again. At first, he could talk, now he doesn't even know his parents."

Runner was silent, unable to say a word, though he was thinking. *Albert was right all the time about me wanting revenge. Someone had to pay for this horrible slaughter and why not the Comanche. Wasn't Raven a Comanche? What if I had been successful in getting the army at the fort to attack these people? My actions would have been just as bad as Raven's, maybe more so.*

Red Cloud was speaking to Runner and he was not hearing.

"Runner," Albert spoke loud and brought him back to the conversation. "The chief asked you a question. Do you want to check their horse herd to verify what he told you?"

"No, Albert, I know he is telling the truth. Deep down I always knew Red Cloud. I am sorry and I ask you and your chiefs' forgiveness for my accusations."

The Comanche chiefs accepted the apology and promised they would find those who killed so many of the already small band of Utes.

"We will let you know when we have them," the Chief Red Cloud promised.

On their trip home, Runner was almost his old self. He continued to tell Albert how sorry he was about his actions the last few months.

"Thank you, my friend, for helping me. I now see the difference between hurting and anger. I will try and be more careful in the future, and I would like for you to tell me more about your God."

In the three days of casual riding back to Runner's village, Albert declared the Gospel to him, about Christ, the Son of God, and how he died for the sins of mankind. Then God's plan of salvation and the work of the Holy Spirit.

"This is a lot to think about, Albert. You are a good man and I see you different than before."

Albert left saying he would come again soon and they would talk more of the things of God.

Molly was ecstatic when he shared the story of what happened.

"It is amazing to watch God work in these kinds of situations, darling. I believe Runner will be alright now. We will keep close contact with him and his people."

The population of Denver continued to grow and so did the Church. The second new addition was added on to meet the needs of the growth.

The sixth grade was no challenge for Bo. The teacher, Mr. Hibbit, let him borrow his guides when he realized Bo's exceptional abilities to learn. The newly elected school board, under pressure from the city council, made plans to start construction on a new and much larger school building, teaching classes from the first through the eleventh grades.

"Pastor, guess you know a new church is under way in the north part of town," Carl said.

"I know, Carl, the new Reverend Watts and I have already met and discussed his desire to start another church. There is a need for another. We can hardly provide for the amount of people we already have, and more move to town every day."

Molly, Albert, and Bo doted on Phillip who, like the town,

seemed to grow daily. Instead of walking, he ran everywhere he went. "He sure wants to get to where he's going in a hurry," Bo remarked. "Do all babies do that?"

"All are different. Each develops their own way of doing things," Molly answered.

At the end of another school year, Bo was at the head of his class and helping Mr. Hibbit teach the first and second graders. He, Albert and Molly, whom he now called his parents, made several trips to his people's village during the year. There were twenty Ute Indians in all who had survived the attack and only five of them were children.

The first day school was out, Bo asked his parents if it would be alright if he could spend the next three months with his people at the village.

"I want to teach them how to read and write. There is no one there now who can do this."

They thought it a splendid idea for him to do this and said they would be glad to purchase any materials he needed. It took the rest of the day gathering supplies and early the next morning with a fully loaded packhorse, they headed for the village.

"Do you really think this is a good idea?" Runner asked after Bo explained what he wanted to do.

"I think it is something we have to do if we are to survive as a tribe. At least let's give it a try."

All twenty were called to a meeting to see what the majority wanted to do about Bo teaching the children to read and write the white man's language. Only a few of the older ones who were taught years ago could speak and understand some English.

"Not only the children," Bo spoke up, "all of us need to know if there is to be a future for us."

Some thought the children would lose their Indian culture if they learned the white man's ways and wanted no part in it.

"We will not forget we are Ute Indians and we will not forget our ways. It will not hurt us to learn other things which will help us in the future."

All of the children wanted to be like Bo. They thought him to be special because he knew the things they wanted to know. Only a couple, who feared the white man's ways, refused to give it a try. The children were ready to start immediately and Bo wasted no time. A shady place under a large cottonwood tree next to the creek was chosen for the classroom. The three-foot square blackboard was placed on an easel with the children sitting on the ground. Bo started his school. At only thirteen, he was the youngest teacher in all of Colorado.

"Do you really think this is a good thing, Albert?" Runner was still skeptical.

"I do. Bo is much wiser than his years, Runner. He can see the future of the Indian nations much clearer than most. He told Molly and I on the way out here if the Indians don't learn like the rest of the world, they would become extinct in a matter of time. Hasn't it helped you over the years to know our language."

"Maybe I should learn to read and write as well as speak."

"I, as well as Bo, would like to see all of you in his school."

The first day of school was a success and when evening came, Bo was ready to call it a day.

The next day, the children and half of the grown-ups were waiting for their teacher. Albert, Molly, and Phillip left for Denver.

The next Sunday, Albert was in his study at the church when Robert, Carl's son, came by and wanted to talk to him. Albert knew immediately what was on his mind.

"Pastor, I really believe the Lord is wanting me to preach. Nothing interests me except reading the Bible and praying. I know Papa wants me to work with him in the store, but this is not what I want and he doesn't understand. Do you?"

"Yes, Robert, I fully understand. I went through the same thing you are dealing with when I felt the call from the Lord. Tell you what, you prepare a message for Sunday. Pray about it and Molly and I will pray also. If you still want to preach, you will have your chance."

Robert walked to his father's store with his mind at peace

for the first time since he announced his call to preach. Then he was afraid he would not be able to say a word when standing before the congregation. He started to go back and tell his pastor more time was needed to think about this. *No, I am sure of this and God will be with me. Reverend Albert says pray about a situation, make sure it is the right thing, and then do it and God will bless. I know without a doubt this is what I am called by God to do*, he thought.

Albert told Molly what he and Robert talked about and asked her to pray the Lord's will be done. "No one but us will know in case he changes his mind. Remember, darling, when the Lord was dealing with me? I didn't know what was going on. The only thing that mattered was to read the Bible and those sermon outlines of your grandfather's. If you don't mind, let Robert study those outlines. They were a great help to me."

Molly brought the sermons to Robert and asked him to study and take care of them because they were very special to her.

Each evening, he would read them and pray for the Lord to give him the right message to preach. By Sunday, he was ready and asked his pastor to pray with him. No one, not even his parents, knew he was going to preach his first sermon.

Carl led in the congregational singing and sang a heartfelt special, then it was time for Albert to preach. He stood and motioned for Robert to join him up front.

"We have a surprise for you this morning," Albert said placing his hand on Robert's shoulder. "This young man you all know. He grew up in this church. The Lord has been dealing with him for some time now to preach his Word. We are going to give him this opportunity to share with us what God has placed on his heart."

His father stood for a moment and started to say something then changed his mind when Albert shook his head no.

Robert was not in the least bit nervous. He stood behind the pulpit and opening his Bible, looked at the people for a few seconds before speaking.

His father had known Robert wanted to be a preacher but his mother had not. She was in total shock as were many of the others.

"I realize my being up here may be a surprise to you, it sort of is to me also. I know I am only sixteen but the Lord has called me to preach his Word. Our pastor and I have been talking and praying about this for a while now and we thought this is a good time to start. Mrs. Molly loaned me some of her grandfather's sermon outlines and one of them will be what I speak on today. It deals with the Holy Spirit of God.

Go back with me about two years ago when Reverend Anderson came to town. The doors and windows to our church were nailed closed. Church services were being held in our homes because the evil forces in our town were in charge. Remember? We prayed God would send someone here to help us. When our pastor and Mrs. Molly asked why the church was boarded up, I felt this could be the answer to our prayer. He didn't look like a preacher, more like a mountain man. He told Papa to let the people know services were to be held the next day. Most of us were here the next morning to see what was going to happen. Reverend Anderson kicked the bottom two boards loose and with his bare hands and he jerked the others off. Then our people began helping him and soon all the windows were letting the cool air in. He told us he had been praying for some time for the Holy Spirit to show him what to do. I can picture him now, behind the pulpit with his Bible and pistol. Do you think the Holy Spirit knew he was going to need both of them?

When we face the workers of iniquity, God will give us what we need to get the job done. Then before he had time to open his Bible, them three hired ruffians came inside God's house to club him and probably us also. He shot the club out of the first man's hand and before anyone knew what was happening, he had them piled in the street out cold. The Spirit of God answered our prayers and his at the same time.

We, as God's children, are challenged every day by evil

forces and were it not for the Holy Spirit, we would be in serious trouble. None of us knows what is in store for us in the days to come, but God does. To me it just makes sense to rely on him to show us the way and follow his leadership. Let us remember, we don't face our opposition alone. Jesus tells us he will not leave or forsake us but will be with us at all times. Again, I thank you for giving me this opportunity to speak."

"I have nothing to add to what Robert has said this morning," Albert stated when Robert went and sat by his parents who were beaming with pride over their son. "Pray for this young man for I know he is going to need your prayers, just as I do."

The congregation also took pride in one of their own surrendering to the ministry and promised to lift him up in their prayers.

CHAPTER FOURTEEN

Time passed quickly the next four years. Denver continued to grow at a rapid pace. Another new school building was built to keep up with the population explosion. Bo excelled in school and helped teach the younger students because teachers were hard to come by. During the three-month vacation from school, he continued to teach his people; most of the children and some of the grown-ups learned to read and write. Chief Red Cloud of the Comanche agreed to loan several of his best Appaloosa horses to the Utes so they could continue to raise their spotted ponies if they would move back to where they used to live. "It is not good for your people to live near the white soldiers." The move was hard for them at first, when they saw all the graves of their loved ones. The new site for the village was across the river from their previous one. Runner, who was now their chief, and another brave were given Comanche wives.

Little Phillip, who was not so little anymore, was six years old and going to school, following in his big brother, Bo's, footsteps. The church Albert pastored was also in a new building program with Robert as Assistant Pastor.

Everything was good and moving forward when tragedy struck. When the first sick people arrived early one morning at the hospital, the four doctors were not alarmed. They all had the same symptoms; a high fever, very sick and dehydrated. By mid-morning, over twenty came or were brought in. Three were in a coma. This was when the doctors became scared. They knew there was something seriously wrong, maybe an epidemic of some kind. The three in a coma died during the afternoon, and the hospital could not keep up with the amount of sick and dying. When the news became known, many families left town for fear they would be the next to die. They did nothing but expose the sickness to other places. The next day, an epidemic was declared and no one was allowed to leave town, though some slipped away during the night.

The hospital asked for volunteers to help with the sick. Bo and Phillip were told to stay home and keep the doors locked while Albert and Molly helped at the hospital. Molly could not believe the number of sick people. The suffering of the ill and their loved ones trying to care for them and those who did not make it brought tears to her eyes. She had never seen anything like this. One out of three who were brought in died and many others died at home. Even the doctors did not know what caused it and did not have any medicine to treat them. The third day, fewer people came down with 'the sickness', as they called it. Over one hundred people died and men kept busy with their shovels night and day burying the dead.

The fourth day, after many hours with hardly any rest, Albert and Molly sat on the front steps of the hospital exhausted. "Darling, I think I need to go check on the boys," Albert said.

"I was thinking the same thing, but wait just a few minutes before you go," she said as she leaned against Albert and placed her head on his neck.

"I am so tired, just sit with me."

Albert knew instantly she was burning up with the fever. He had cared for many during the last few days that felt just like she did.

"Darling, we have to get you inside. You have the fever."

She never heard a word he said as her life slipped away while in his arms.

Many had died with this sickness but none so near to Albert and the boys as Molly, the beloved wife and mother. Each of them knew their life would never be the same without her. Albert could barely see for the tears as he stumbled his way home. "No, I'll do it myself," he told the burial detail when they offered to perform the last rights. His question to God was, "Why, God, did you have to take my Molly just now?" This he repeated while he gently carried her the few blocks to their home. Phillip and Bo thought she was asleep when Albert kicked his foot softly against the door. He placed her gently on their bed and pulled a blanket over her without saying a word to the boys. He motioned them to follow him into the living room, of which Molly had been so fond.

"Sit down, please," he said after closing the door. "Something dreadful has happened. Your mother contracted the sickness and is gone to be with the Lord. She passed away only a few minutes ago." He paused, waiting for what he said to sink in. Bo was quick to understand, but Phillip just looked questionably at Albert. He sat on the sofa and placed Phillip in his lap. "Son, your mother died like so many of the other people from the fever. She gave her life caring for the others. I know you don't understand now, neither do I. We will have to do the best we can in dealing with this. It will not be easy, but with God's help, we will get through this." Albert placed his strong arms around the boys and all three shed their tears as Albert prayed for God to give them the strength they would need now and in the future. He also prayed for the other families who had lost loved ones. He knew his work would be cut out for him for days to come, helping to console the many bereaved in Denver.

When his church congregation heard the sad news about Molly, they all came to do what they could to help. Several of the ladies washed and dressed her in one of her favorite dresses and when they finished, Molly looked as though she was sleeping peacefully.

"The boys and I are going up on the mountain to bury Molly where she was raised. This is what she wanted. I thank all of you for what you have done and we will come back in a couple of weeks if things go right."

Before daylight the next morning, Albert and the boys left Denver, Albert driving the wagon with Phillip and Bo riding behind. Dap followed close to the wagon seeming to know all was not right. The beautiful casket Carl gave as a gift was wrapped in oilcloth in case of rain. It being the middle of June, the wild flowers covered the mountainside and the creeks running full from the melting snow. They had made this trip many times before as a complete family, never dreaming of something like this. Two young strong horses pulled the wagon without seeming to tire and half the distance was covered by dark the first day.

Bo and Phillip prepared a quick meal by campfire light and Albert tended the horses while listening to the conversation between the boys.

"I can't believe Mother is dead," Phillip was saying.

"I know, it seems like a bad dream," Bo answered. "I guess there are lots of people feeling the same way. Two of the kids I teach in school, Jimmy and Ellen, were of the first to die from the awful sickness."

"Bo, Papa didn't say much today. Do you think he is alright?"

"I think so. He is just grieving. God will talk to him and he will feel better soon. How are you doing, little brother?"

"Alright. I just feel empty inside knowing I will never see her again."

Before going to sleep, Albert quoted the Twenty-third Psalm. "I feel the same as you boys do, but with time, it will get better. The Lord says he will always be with us, to comfort and care for each of us. We will talk about Molly and her death over the next weeks. It will help us find closure."

The next day was the same, breaking camp early and covering several miles before daybreak. They entered the large meadows three hours before dark. When the cabin was in sight, Phillip called out excitedly, "Look, Papa, there's Whitey!"

The white buffalo calf Albert and Molly saw seven years ago was now a very large bull. He and a few cows returned to this place every spring to spend the summer grazing on the lush mountain grass. He had no fear of these people and would let

Molly pet him as his old father would. When they stopped at the barn, the white buffalo walked up to the wagon and sniffed the coffin. He then shook his head from side to side and let out several loud bellows.

"He knows," Bo said. "Listen to him. He grieves just like us."

"Yes Son, Whitey loved your mother. He would stand and let her pet him for hours. Never have I seen a wild animal do such a thing."

After the supplies were taken care of, Albert, with the help of the boys, cooked a light meal and talked of previous times up here on the mountain.

"Tell us again, Papa, when you first saw Mother," Phillip asked.

"I was real sick with a high fever from being mauled by a mountain lion; the same lion which had killed her father. I was in the bed over there against the wall and I sort of remember her bathing my face with a cool wash cloth thinking she had to be an angel. If it were not for her, I could have died. She doctored me back to health, bless her."

"The old lion was a mean one, wasn't he Papa? He makes a soft rug now though."

The boys never tired of hearing the many stories about Albert and Molly.

"Where are we going to bury Mother?" Bo asked.

"Near the big rock in the aspen grove next to the creek. That was her favorite place up here. Even when she was a little girl, she played there for hours. She told me she would sit on the rock and study her lessons her father taught and wonder about how it would be to live where there were a lot of people. She and I sat there many times and I told her stories of my boyhood back in England. That is where we will place her and when it's my turn, I want you boys to bury me beside her."

The boys were asleep when Albert went back out to the barn where Molly lay in her coffin. "Darling, only with help from God will I be able to get through this. It will be hard on the boys, especially Phillip being so young. You are no longer in this body, but if you can hear me, I want to tell you I loved you with all my heart and still do. You were my right hand in everything I undertook. A perfect pastor's wife, a perfect mother and the best part of my life. Our time together wasn't near long enough. I feel a great loss now with your passing even though I know God is still with me. In the morning, we will place your body in your favorite spot here on the mountain, but you will be in my heart forever."

The horses woke Albert from a troubled sleep in the early hours of morning wanting to be fed. He turned them into the large corral where they could drink from the creek and eat their fill then picked out two shovels and a pick and went to the burial site knowing each of the boys would want to help with their mother's grave. The ground was still hard but gave way to the powerful thrust of Albert driving the pick deep into the soil. The boys, hearing Albert at work, were soon there to do their part. He wanted them to always remember helping with this awful chore. One day they would do this for him.

The white barked aspen thicket next to the outcrop of black granite boulders with the creek splashing was indeed a most beautiful sight and sound.

"I can see why Mother loved this place," Bo said.

"Papa, could we live here like you and Mother did? I mean all the time?" Phillip chimed in.

"That would be nice, Son, if I didn't have the responsibility of preaching. I don't know if the Lord would permit such a thing. I guess we might pray about it though."

One of the horses was hitched to a homemade wooden sled and the casket brought to the site. A rope tied to each end made it easy to let the casket down, Albert on one end and both the boys on the other.

Albert was surprised when Phillip asked if he could read Psalms twenty-three.

He handed Phillip the Bible and told him Molly would be proud of him. He hardly needed the Bible because Molly had taught him to recite this and many more scriptures.

"Do either of you want to say something?" Albert asked them.

"I miss you, Mama," Bo said with tears running down his cheeks.

"Why did you call her Mama, Bo?" Phillip asked.

"Because she wasn't really my mother, but she was my mama all these years. She liked it when I called her mama."

Phillip asked Albert if he could call her mama.

"Yes, Son, you can call her mama also. I don't know why we didn't teach you to do that."

Phillip looked down at the casket and spoke. "Mama, you told me about my real mother and father. I liked the stories about them and wish I could remember them. You and Papa are the only parents I know and now you are gone to be with God. I love you, Mama, and I promise to always remember you." After he said this, he grabbed Albert by the leg and cried.

"It's alright, Son. You did good and maybe she heard what you said. We all miss her terribly and one day we will be with her again. Molly was the best part of our lives but we still have each other and God. He will see us through the hard times to come."

The grave was filled and wild flowers were dug and planted over it. They spent most of the day making a cross and carving her name and dates on it.

"This will do for now, boys. When we get back to town, Carl will order us one carved out of stone."

"Now none of us has had a good meal for a week and I am kind of hungry. What say we cook us up something like Molly would? You boys can get the rifle and go kill a young buck while I start with the other stuff."

Albert heard the rifle sound before he had a fire built. He smiled and said aloud, "Thank you, Lord, for the time I had with my darling Molly. Guide me and the boys in the way you would have us go."

While eating they discussed going to the top of the

mountain the next day. It was only a three-hour climb and they could see for miles in three directions. They would pack a lunch and leave early come morning.

There was still snow in places where the sun did not reach and it was too tempting to resist a snowball fight. The two boys against Albert about evened out, maybe a little in their favor. Albert was delighted the boys could laugh and have fun at a time like this; it was what Molly would want for them.

"Look there, Phillip," Bo said, pointing towards the southeast. That is where my people, the small band of Utes live. One day soon I will go and visit with them. My mother and father are buried there along with my best friend, your father, Bogie."

"Tell me again how fast he could run with a wooden leg and about teaching you to run and do flips. Do you think I could run as fast as you if I had a wooden leg?"

"If you practice you could run just as fast as I can, maybe even faster."

The clouds began rolling in and the wind began to blow. They quickly mounted their horses and started down the mountain, wanting to get home before the storm caught them. They did not make it.

"Stay close," Albert yelled, hardly able to be heard over the howling wind and thunder. The rain stopped as quickly as it started and a wet heavy snow began to fall before they reached the barn.

The horses were unsaddled and dried with sacks then fed before they made their way to the cabin. Albert taught them early on to take care of their animals first before doing anything else.

"This has been a good day," Albert said while sitting with the boys and drinking a hot cup of tea in front of a crackling fire. They were all wishing Molly was with them.

"What are we going to do tomorrow?" Phillip asked.

"I don't know, Son, maybe we'll plant a garden. I realize it won't do much if we are not here to tend it but it will produce

some. It will give us an excuse to make this trip more often."
This pleased Phillip and Bo. Every spring they planted one in
Denver because Molly insisted they do so. Not only for
themselves but also for them who were not able.

It took a week to prepare the soil and plant. When it was
done, Albert prayed they have a bountiful harvest.

Two days later, Phillip ran to where Albert and Bo were
working on the corral fence saying someone was riding towards
the cabin.

"Don't get much company up here. Did you recognize
them?"

"They were too far away, Papa."

There were two riders and one was a woman. When they
came nearer, Bo said it was Runner and his wife.

They rode up to the cabin where the three Andersons
awaited them.

"This is a good surprise," Albert said as he offered to help
the woman dismount.

"Hello, friend Albert. It is good to see you also. I would like
for you to meet my wife, Rain, and son, Cub."

"Bo told me you had gotten married, though not about a
baby."

"Cub is just four months old, maybe he didn't know."

"You must be tired. It is not an easy climb to get up here.
Let's go inside and rest while my boys take your horses to the
barn and care for them, then we will find something to eat."

Runner and his small family had gone to Denver to see
Albert and Molly. When they got there, they were told of the
terrible sickness and death, which devastated Denver, and of
Molly passing.

"We had to come and see if there was something we could
do for you."

"Thanks, my friend. Just coming here shows how much you
care. There is nothing anyone can do, it will just take time."

After enjoying a good meal, the men went outside to talk so
Rain could suckle her baby and rest on the bed.

"Albert, there is something else I want to tell you and your boys. The Comanche caught Raven. Chief Red Cloud sent word to me to come and see my enemy. You know how much I hated him for what he did. When I saw him, it made me sick to see what they did to him. I actually felt sorry for him. The whole tribe held an open council because they said he shamed the whole Comanche Nation. Some wanted to skin him alive but decided he would die too quickly. They turned him over to the women to punish him. They split his tongue because he could not tell the truth, calling him forked tongue. They hamstrung his right foot so he will always have to use a crutch to get around. Then they cut him in a way he could never have any children, the women said his offspring would most likely be like him. While I was there, they put him on an old horse and told him if any Comanche found him after ten days, they would let the women work on him some more. I would rather have been skinned alive. I just wanted you and the boys to know he has been dealt with."

After hearing this, Albert agreed he had been dealt with. To live the rest of his life in such a condition would be awful, plus, the fear of someone finding him and taking him back to be cut on again.

"Enough horror for now," Albert commented. "I want to get a better look at those horses you were riding. I have never seen better looking animals anywhere."

The spotted Appaloosa horses were descendants from the ones Chief White Wolf, Bo's father, raised. Raven and his band stole them the day of the Ute slaughter.

"The Comanche have been good to us, Albert. I shudder to think I tried to get the army to attack and kill innocent people. If it were not for you, it is no telling what I would have done. Thank you for making me face the truth."

"That is what friends are for, Runner. One thing I want to know, have you thought any more about Jesus, the Son of God?"

"To be truthful, I have, and I want to know more about him.

Come and see me sometime and we will talk."

Bo asked Runner if he could travel with him when he went back to his village. He said he and Rain would be delighted for the company and asked Albert if he and Phillip wanted to come also.

"I guess it has been a while since I last saw your people. I'll leave it up to Phillip."

"Can we, Papa? I have never been to where they live now."

"Only when you were a baby," Albert said. "They moved back to their old village where the massacre took place when your parents were killed."

"Is it safe to stay there?" Phillip asked.

"It is as safe as any place," Runner answered. "One never knows what tomorrow holds, but don't be afraid little friend, your papa will be there with you."

The return trip was planned in two days. This would give them another day to rest and visit. Rain did not have much to say because she knew very little English. When Bo finally realized this, his teaching instinct took over. He could speak the Comanche language fairly well and before long, they were in conversation. He promised to teach her enough English so she could understand. This made her happy. All day they sat and talked both in her language and in English.

The wagon which was used to haul the coffin was left in the barn along with most of the supplies. They decided the two wagon horses would have to go with them. "We will be coming back in a few weeks to work the garden," Albert promised.

In the afternoon of the second day, they came to the narrow ledge where there was just enough room for one horse to be led. It was about two miles long and in some places, very steep.

"We have made this trip when the snow covered everything," Albert said when he saw how frightened Rain was.

"I will go first, the two wagon horses next, then Bo. Runner will be next with the baby. Rain, you and Phillip can stay here. When we get off the ledge, I will come back for you, just wait for me. I should be back in about three hours."

Phillip wanted to go in the first group, then decided Rain could not stay by herself. Albert let Dap lead the way and he led the first of the wagon horses. They did not much like walking the ledge at first but calmed down after a while. It took an hour and a half to where the path opened to a grassy meadow.

"Picket these two horses and let Dap run loose. If you will, set up camp. I am going back to get Rain and Phillip. Albert ran at his mile-eating trot and soon found he was not in the best condition. "I used to be able to run uphill for hours at a time," he muttered to himself. "I'll have to work on it." It took most of an hour to run the two miles.

Rain and Phillip were patiently waiting for his return. "Now it's your turn," he told them. "If you want, both of you can ride and I will lead. Rain, you first and then Bo. Don't be afraid, the horses know what to do, sit tight and relax. You don't have to look down, look at the rock side."

Albert talked to Rain for the first mile then she started to calm down. "Molly and I walked this ledge several times. Phillip, your mother and father came up this same path to get married."

"I remember Mama telling me the story. It makes this special to me, Papa."

When they were nearing the end of the path, Albert motioned them to look to the west. The sun had just dipped below the horizon and the clouds were ablaze with a deep red. Supper was waiting for them and a warm fire soon took the chill away.

"We have made good time these first two days and the rest of the way should be easier," Albert stated.

They were sitting around the campfire and Rain walked off to nurse the baby. "Runner, why do you call her Rain?" Phillip asked.

"Rain is her name. Indians name their children after events and sometimes after animals. I was told before she was born, it hardly rained for over two years. The day she was born, it rained hard from daylight till dark, more rain than they could ever remember so they called her Rain. She says still when it is dry for a long time, they ask her to pray for rain. Sometimes it rains and sometimes it doesn't. They named me Runner because when I was little I never walked. I ran everywhere I went. As a small boy, I could outrun most men in the village. Do you find this strange?"

"Not since you told me. I think it is a good way to name someone."

Everyone was ready to go when morning arrived, even the horses. By noon, the foothills were behind them. The prairie was abloom with every color you could think of, the air fresh and the creeks and streams clear and cold from the melting snow. Three days from the time they left the cabin, they entered the Ute village. As usual, extra teepees were erected and Albert and his boys were given the biggest one. Phillip had grown so much, no one knew who he was. In no time, he felt at home and playing with the few children. All the grown men and women knew Bogie and Singing Dove, and when they told them Molly had died, they could not believe it. What would Albert, the preacher man, do without her?"

Four days passed and Albert said it was time he went back to Denver. Bo wanted to stay for a few more weeks and teach his people, especially Rain.

CHAPTER FIFTEEN

It was after dark when Albert and Phillip arrived back in Denver. They stabled the horses and entered their house through the back door. The emptiness was almost unbearable for them. Albert lit the lamp which Molly always kept full of oil and ready for use, and started to prepare something to eat.

"Papa, I think I am going to bed. Don't fix me anything."

"I was thinking the same, Son. We will just wait until morning and cook us a good breakfast. If you want, I'll tuck you in like we used to do."

Phillip said he would like that and Albert sat on the bed as Phillip dressed into his nightclothes.

"Son, I know you miss your mother as much as I do. I can never take her place, but together with the help of the Lord, we will make it."

Albert made it to the door before Phillip spoke.

"I know, Papa. Goodnight."

The ladies of the church had cleaned every room in the house and everything was as Molly always kept it.

"Darling, I miss you more right now than ever," Albert said as he looked at her picture sitting on the dresser. "This house feels so empty without you."

The next morning, Albert made his rounds visiting the church people who were excited he was back. Robert had done an excellent job filling in the last three Sundays was expressed by all. At Carl's mercantile, he found Robert working with his father.

"Robert, I want to thank you for doing such a splendid job

while I was gone."

"Enjoyed every minute of it, pastor. There is something I would like to talk to you about."

They went into a small room in back of the store which had an office sign on the door.

"Pastor, do you think there are enough people here to build another church. I realize I lack experience, but I feel the need to be a full-time pastor. I want to know what you think I should do."

"I know exactly how you feel, Robert. I experienced the same feelings, and yes, there are enough people here. This is certainly something we need to pray about before making a decision."

"I have been praying for some time though I haven't mentioned it to anyone yet."

Both agreed to continue praying for God's answer.

For a month, Albert worked with those who had lost loved ones with the same sickness that had taken Molly's life. He understood their feelings with compassion just as they understood his.

"It will take time to get over this," he said to each of them. "There will always be a vacant spot in our lives."

A month later after service, Albert asked Robert if he had time to talk. He wanted to know if he still felt the call to pastor a church. Ever since he and Phillip entered the vacant house, he also felt he needed a change in his life. Maybe the solitude of the mountain would be the place for him and Phillip now. If Bo would consider coming with them to tutor Phillip in his studies, he could have time to work the garden and collectively get his own life back together.

He explained to Robert his desires and asked if he would be interested in filling his position.

"I don't want to see you leave, pastor. Let's forget about this whole thing."

"Robert, I don't want to leave but this is something I have to do. It will help us both. God answers prayers and there are times we don't understand the way he does it. If he is calling you to be a pastor, this is your answer. I don't know yet what he has for me, but in time I will know."

Reluctantly, Robert agreed and was asked not to mention this to anyone until Albert gave the church his resignation. Of course, the boys were excited they would spend time on the mountain and could hardly keep it to themselves.

When Albert stood behind the podium the next Sunday and gave his resignation, no one was able to speak. They could not believe what they heard. He began to give the reasons for this decision. Most of the women began to weep. When he revealed what he and Robert had been praying about, Robert being called to pastor a church, the people began to understand. They would still have a pastor they all could depend on to preach the Word in truth.

After an emotional service, a picnic was planned and many who were not church members, but close friends of Albert, came to wish him the best. Over two hundred people came, each assuring him if he ever needed anything, they would see he got it. He was offered money by many but Albert refused it. "I have no use for money where I am going. The mountain has everything I need."

"How long are we going to stay in the cabin this time?" Phillip asked excitedly as they were packing the last items on one of the pack animals.

"I can't rightly say, Son. When it's time to leave, we will know. It could be a few days or a year."

Phillip was hoping for a year. There was so much more to do there then in Denver. Bo had warned him classes would take as much of his time up on the mountain as it did in town. Phillip was a fast learner, especially in math. One of the pack-horses was packed mostly with books and other school supplies.

The climb became harder as they moved higher up the mountain. The animals were in good physical condition and had no problems. Early afternoon, Albert called for a rest stop. "We don't have to hurry, boys. The weather looks to be fine so let's take our time on this trip."

"I have noticed more wagon tracks on the road this morning than usual," Bo commented.

"I noticed it as well. Carl said he has been selling a lot of things to people who are looking for gold up here though I haven't heard of any being found."

The third morning, Albert and the boys were crossing a stream when someone called out to them. Two men were panning for gold a little ways up the creek. One of the men was a big man much larger than Albert, the other a boy about the age of Bo.

"Where you going?" the big man asked.

"Up to our cabin," Albert answered.

The men stopped their work and came to where Albert was.

"Better be careful if you talking about the cabin ten or so miles further up on this trail which has a garden out front. There's an Indian with his squaw and little one lives there and said no one was allowed within ten miles of his place. He has a gun and knows how to use it. He shot my pick handle clean off the other day."

"Thanks for the warning, friend. If it's who I think it is, he's a mean one for sure. You better listen to him."

"Who do you think it is, Papa?" Phillip asked when they were out of hearing distance of the two men.

"Has to be Runner and his family, Son. I wonder what he's up to."

The last ten miles took them four hours. Runner and Rain were working in the garden when they got there. Cub, their six-month-old baby lay in the shade of a large ponderosa pine close by.

"Don't you two have anything better to do than spend your time out in this hot sun hoeing weeds in someone else's garden?"

Runner said he expected them a week earlier. Rain insisted they come and help with the vegetable garden and cutting the hay. "I don't know how but she knew you would be coming soon."

Phillip and Bo tended the horses while Albert and Runner talked.

"We came across two men a few miles back who told us there was a crazy Indian up here. They were panning for gold."

"Must be the two we run off when we got here. They set up camp here in your cabin. The place was a mess when we arrived. It took two days to clean things. The big man threatened to bash Rain's head in with his pick if she didn't cook for them. I wanted to shoot him but shot his pick handle instead."

The three men and Phillip worked in the garden late while Rain prepared a great meal which was greatly enjoyed. Runner and Rain moved into the room Bogie and Singing Dove built in the large barn several years earlier. The door had been locked when they left and had not been used for a long time. They had spent the winter with Albert and Molly after Albert married them.

The vegetables were coming in by the bushels. The summers were short up on the mountain but with the bright sunny days and the warm fertile soil, the plants grew to maturity fast. Soon the root cellar was filled with canned and dehydrated food. Bo and Phillip killed several deer which were cured and hung in the cold cellar along with the other food.

It was the last of August when the food gathering was over and the men started cutting the high protein mountain grass for hay. After working hard for two days, they were surprised when Carl, Robert, and four more of the churchmen from Denver drove up with three wagons filled with grain for the horses and other needed supplies. "Thought you could use this if you stay the winter up here. There's sugar, flour, cornmeal and other stuff you can't grow," Carl said. "You sure you want to stay on this mountain all winter?"

"We are planning to unless the Lord says different. I thank you for all you brought us. It will come in handy when the cold comes."

Whitey, the white buffalo, came ambling up while they were talking and Phillip went up to him and scratched his face. The men were amazed at such a sight.

"Unbelievable," Robert said. "How did you train him to be so tame?"

Albert related the story of the father of this buffalo and what happened to him. Then this one was born the next spring after his father was killed. Molly had no trouble making a pet out of both.

"You should have seen him cry and greave when we brought Mama up here to be buried," Phillip stated. "He watched when we had her funeral."

Robert asked if he could pet Whitey. "He probably doesn't care if you do it easy."

Carl saw the hay had been cut and was curing on the ground. "We can give you a few days' work if you want."

The offer was gladly accepted and no time was wasted. They now had ten men instead of four. Phillip offered to help Rain with preparing the meals and caring for little Cub.

At the end of three days, stacks of hay dotted the two large meadows and the large barn was filled to capacity.

"This should last us through the winter, men," Albert told them when they stopped for the day. "When the snow starts getting deep, the grass-eating animals leave the higher parts of the mountain. With the grain and food you men brought and this much hay, the horses and us should fare well. Thank you so much for your thoughtfulness, and tell the church the same for us."

The next morning, the church crew left for home and Runner stayed two more days.

"We would like for you to stay the winter with us," Albert offered.

"You know this mountain doesn't like Indians up here in the winter time, my white friend. We just wanted to be a little help to you and the boys. You have done so much for us. We will look for you come spring. By then, there may be a couple of spotted ponies waiting for Phillip and Bo, and for you also, Albert, if you want one."

"I'll wait a while for mine. Dap still has a lot of good years left, I hope. Grandfather bought him for me when I turned sixteen and he has been with me since then. I hate to think about not having him around."

The next morning, Runner and his family left. He told Albert when they came to the village, he would be ready to talk to him about God. "Rain and I have been talking and we want to know more of him," he said.

Albert promised as soon as it was safe to travel, they would see them. Three days later, it snowed and Albert, the mountain man, put on his leather clothing as did the boys and they spent the winter by themselves on the mountain. Bo and Phillip worked many long days reading and studying. Bo was an excellent teacher and Phillip an apt student. Before going to bed, Albert would read the scriptures and they would talk about what they meant. Most days, before the snow covered everything, they would go the short distance to Molly's grave and spend time talking about her and the things she had done.

One of the things they liked best was when Albert would tell of his family back in England, of the castle where his grandfather lived and of the huge city of London. It was hard for the boys to imagine thousands of people in one place. They found pictures of castles and wanted to know if Grandfather's castle was big.

"It is as big and bigger than most. There are rooms I have never been in. When I was a boy, they told stories about the dungeon where scary things happened. At night, you could hear sounds like someone moaning and other weird noises."

"Papa, can we go there one day and see for ourselves where you lived?"

"Molly and I were planning to go when you got a little older, Phillip. She wanted to see where I grew up and meet my family. I often think of them and would like to see them again. Maybe we will plan to go in the near future. Yes, we will go back to England to see our family."

The winter on the mountain was mild compared to some. Albert taught the boys how to make snowshoes, though Bo's had to be altered so as to fit his wooden leg. At first, he had a little trouble but soon he could walk as fast as the other two. The chore that took the most time was keeping the horses watered. The creek froze almost solid. On sunny days, the horses were let out of the barn and they would eat the snow. On the days they had to be kept inside, snow had to be melted. Jim Butcher, Molly's father, built the barn and cabin and he built well. It did not take much to keep them warm. The rigorous work and play, tending horses and keeping the path from house to barn shoveled, kept them busy. The good fresh food and exercise made their bodies strong.

Albert was usually the first to get up. He heated water and had tea ready for Phillip and Bo, then he would go to the barn and let the horses out if it was a good day. This was his time to pray. "Lord, sometimes I feel I should be back in Denver preaching. If I were, Robert would not be doing what you called him to do. I know you have a job for me somewhere telling people about you. Is it to preach to Runner and his tribe? He asked if I would go and talk to him this spring and I plan to. Some think preaching to Indians is a waste of time, though I know different. You died for them same as you did for all. Help me, Lord, to do what is right. Show me your will, and Lord, I would like to go back to England and see my family. Amen."

March came and the snows came less frequently. The days were a little warmer melting the snow and ice. "Three or four more weeks, boys, and we may be able to head for the Ute village."

Though they immensely enjoyed the mountain, all were ready for a change. The creek began to run during the day and almost freeze again at night. When the first of the wild flowers bloomed, Albert said it was time to go so they packed the horses and headed off the mountain. There was still ice on the narrow trail and Albert slowly led them safely to the bottom. It was much warmer now than on the mountain. The grass came almost to the horses' bellies and wildlife seemed to be everywhere.

"The village where we are going is the place my real parents lived, isn't it, Papa?"

"Yes, Son, your real mother and father lived there and it is where renegades slaughtered them."

"I remember you and Mama telling me the story of that day of how most of the people in the village were killed."

"I remember also," Bo added. "Your father, Bogie, was my best friend. He made my first wooden leg and taught me to walk and run like him. I believe he was the last one to get killed. My father was the first. Raven and his killers rode into the village and yelled, "Kill the Chief!" and then shot an arrow through his chest. If it had not been for Albert and Molly, all of us would have died."

"I believe God spared you for a reason," Albert said. "There is a purpose as to why he allows things to happen, though we may never understand."

They traveled in silence for a while, each trying to understand and cope with what had happened almost nine years ago.

The Utes had moved the small village across the river from where it used to be. Bo's father, White Wolf, had been chief before being killed. His teepee was still standing in the middle of the village and was used for visitors. Albert had used it many times. The floor was covered thick with buffalo hides which were tanned and worked until they were soft and flexible. A circle of rocks in the middle was used to build a fire in when it was cold. None of the Indians ever entered it except to clean and air it out.

When Albert and his boys came into sight of the village, they were on a hill several hundred yards away. A herd of twenty some horses were grazing with three young boys watching over them. They were the prized Appaloosa horses raised and trained by the Utes. They only kept the best mares and stallions for breeding. Some were white with black spots, some black, red and mouse colored, with what they called a white blanket on their rump, with spots on the blanket. They had purchased the first ones many years before from their ancestors across the mountains in Utah. Colts of all colors were running and playing like little children.

"Wonder which one will be mine?" Phillip asked watching the young horses run. If I can choose, I will ask for the white one with the most spots. The one standing off by himself watching us," Bo said. "He is the most alert one out there besides the stallion on top of the hill that looks just like him. He is watching us also."

All of a sudden, the spotted stallion gave out a shrill whistle sound and all the horses stopped what they were doing and looked their way as did the boys who were with the horses. Several people in the village were watching them also.

"So much for surprising them," Albert said with a laugh.

Before they reached the village, Runner and two more of the men came to meet them.

"We welcome you, Andersons, to our homes," Runner said. "Glad to see our friends from the mountain."

As usual, the women started immediately preparing a feast for their friends and kin, and what a feast it was. When everyone finished eating, Runner stood and addressed Albert.

"I have talked with our people and told them you will tell us about your all-powerful God. They agreed to hear what you have to say. At first some of them said no, but changed their mind when I told them anyone who could live with the Old Ones' spirits high on the mountain, must have a strong spirit themselves.

"We will hear what you have to say in the morning."

This was a sign the day was over for visiting. Phillip and Bo went directly to bed though Albert walked down to the river to talk to God.

Albert knew what he would say and how he said it, was going to be very important. He also realized no other preacher may ever get such an opportunity to talk to this village again. "God, you have always before given me the right message to preach. Now I call on you to lead me in what to say to these people. They know there is a higher power, but they think it is the spirits of their old ancestors who live on the mountain. Some will listen, though some won't, but isn't this the same with all people?" After making his petition to God, he was at peace knowing everything would be fine.

Phillip and Bo were already gone when Albert woke the next morning. *Bet they're with the boys watching the horses,* he thought. *I cannot blame them. Those are beautiful animals.*

There was a fresh pail of water right outside his door. He washed and refused the food which was offered him. He knew soon the chance to speak to these people would come and he prayed again for spiritual direction. An hour later, all the people assembled themselves under an old oak near the river. Everyone was there sitting on the ground, even the boys who were in charge of the horses. Phillip and Bo were out in front and Albert knew they were there to support him. The passage he chose to speak on was entitled 'The Unknown God,' Acts 17:23.

He began, "First, I thank you for allowing me to speak to you about my God and his Son, Jesus. He is not just my God nor is he just the white man's God. He is the God of anyone who wants him. I want to read to you from his book about a people who lived long ago and didn't know him. They were a real religious people and worshipped many gods, though they didn't know about the God who created the heavens, the earth and everything else. Paul, a preacher, went through their town one day and told them about the one and only God who created all mankind and wanted them all to serve him just as I have come to tell you about him. We are not to worship the sun or rain or spirits, but worship the one who made all things. If you ask him to be your God, he will and his Spirit will live within you. There are many things I want to tell you about him and his Son, Jesus, but it would take a long time. If you want to know more I would be glad to tell you."

They did not know what to make of what was said, so Bo told them he asked the Lord to come into his heart and be his God many years ago and it made a huge difference in his life. Runner, Rain and most of the children said they wanted this God to be their God. A few of the older ones said they would think about it. They wanted to see if it made a difference in these who accepted him. A few said they would keep their old ways; it was good enough for their ancestors.

For several days, Albert and his boys stayed in the village and read to them more of the Word of God and taught them many things concerning their new faith.

When it was time to go, they promised to come again. Albert gave them a Bible he had purchased from Carl and told them to read it every day. "The Holy Spirit will teach you. I wish we could stay longer, Runner, but I and my sons are going back to England. I want them to meet my family and see where I lived before coming here to America."

CHAPTER SIXTEEN

There was a lot of excitement when they told the church congregation in Denver where they were going.

"We will surely be back in several months," Albert said.

They rode their horses part of the time and a coach whenever they could with the horses tied behind. They sold all but Dap when they booked passage on the ship. "This one is not for sale," Albert told the man.

"Give you top dollar for him."

"He is part of the family. Money can't buy him."

Phillip and Bo enjoyed the journey across the vast country. They had only read about the places they traveled through. Then the ocean voyage was unbelievable. Dap did not much care for this part of the trip, though he liked when they would brush and spend time with him. "You are going to see your old home, boy. Hope everyone is well."

Albert had written several letters through the years, though he never received an answer. Most of the passengers hurried topside when land was sighted. *Almost twelve years,* Albert thought as he gazed at the shores of England still more than two miles away. *That makes me thirty-three years of age and Grandfather about eighty-two. Lord, let him be alive. There is so much I must tell him and Father, and I must make amends with Mother. I left them these many years ago thinking only of myself and what I wanted to do. Only a kid about the age of Bo, seeking I don't even know what. All I knew was I had to go to America. Would I have ever come to know you, Lord, if I had stayed here in England, and would Bogie still be alive? I would not have known Molly, and Phillip would not be here.* All these things passed through Albert's mind as he watched the distance close between the ship and England.

"Papa, how far is it to the castle?" Phillip asked, bringing Albert to the present.

"About three hours, Son, but first we have to unload and get our belongings together. We should get there before dark."

The ship slowly made her way through the bay and up to the landing dock as she did so many times before. The sailors wasted no time in getting the walk in place, and the passengers began to leave the ship. A ramp from the lower deck for the livestock was lowered and the horses were led out, Dap being the first. A line of coaches was waiting for passengers who needed transportation. One of the drivers helped load their luggage and Dap was tied behind the coach and they were off to Grandfather's castle.

Albert asked the driver if he knew Lord Anderson and if he was well.

"As for as I know he is. He hardly ever gets out anymore though. You some kind of relation?"

"He's my grandfather and I haven't seen in a number of years."

"Albert was greatly relieved to know Lord Anderson was still living even if he didn't get out much. As they got closer to the castle, Albert began to point out landmarks. They traveled through two small towns which seemed to be bigger than he remembered and new houses where only open pasture used to be. When they entered the Anderson property, everything looked the same as before. He recalled the many times he traveled this lane. Then the house where he grew up came into sight. It was different. Children were playing in the yard, lots of children. Then the castle came in view and Albert stopped the coach. "Look, boys, this is Anderson Castle. Is it as big as you thought it would be? Nothing is changed. The large trees lining the road and the gray stone stables, and see those large stones high up on the hill? That is what we call the 'out-cropping'. I played there many times when I was growing up, so did Grandfather and your father, Phillip. Now you can."

The driver stopped in front of the castle and the huge front door opened. An aged, white-haired man stood there leaning on his black ebony cane. For a minute, he just stood there. Then a broad smile as he leaned his head back and laughed aloud, something he hardly ever did. Another white-haired man appeared and then ran down the steps with open arms. Albert and his father stood there with their arms around each other for a minute. For the first time in his life, he felt the loving compassion of his father's strong arms around him. This is what he wanted as a young person. This is what he came back to England for, his family.

"Your grandfather told me a month ago you were coming home, Son. He saw you in a dream and told me then. He has been doing strange things lately and this is the best yet."

Albert looked up and saw his old grandfather standing with one arm stretched out to him and the other on his cane to keep him from falling. He ran up the steps and hugged his grandfather. "Grandfather, it is so good to see you."

"And good to have you home again, Son. Who are these fine-looking gentlemen you have here with you?"

"The young one shaking hands with Father is your nephew, Phillip Anderson, Bogie's son. The other is almost an adopted son, Bo Anderson. He is a very brilliant young man, Grandfather. We have much to talk about. I have things to tell and I want to know everything that has happened over the last twelve years."

And talk they did. By the time the evening meal was over, it was too dark for Bo and Phillip to explore the castle. They would have to wait until the next day. Albert asked about all the children he saw on the drive to the castle who were at his mother's house.

"We turned it into an orphanage a couple of years after you left," his father said. "It was your mother's idea. She and Miss Margaret became the best of friends and one day approached your grandfather and I about it. They asked if we would take care of the financial part, they would work with the children. As it turned out, we have all been involved in the endeavor. There are twenty some children there, mostly girls, and we had to hire another couple to help with schooling them."

This sparked Bo and young Phillip's interest. They asked if they could go and see what an orphanage was like.

"In the morning, we will go and visit. I want to see my mother," Albert said.

Grandfather promised the best thing to ever happen was when Albert put his mother and Miss Margaret together. At first, there was total chaos. Then somehow, they reached out to one another and became the best of friends.

"I felt terrible doing what I did," Albert stated. "I'm glad it turned out like it did."

"Your mother is a different woman, Albert, nothing like she was when you left. I can almost like her these days."

Phillip and Bo spent the first four hours the next morning exploring the castle while Albert shared some of his life's experiences with his father and grandfather.

When he told of his marriage to Molly and becoming a preacher, they were astounded. Then about the death of Bogie and his Indian wife leaving their six-month-old son, Phillip, for him and Molly to raise. As he told them the story, their hearts began to break with compassion.

"So, Bogie did tell you the truth about him being my brother. I thought he would. He was so mistreated. I'm glad he found someone to love in his later years. I can tell you, this young man will receive his rightful place in the Anderson family, and Bogie will also be listed as a son of my father. The awful lie will no longer exist."

Albert, with his two sons, decided to walk the mile to see his mother. Along the way, he told the boys some of his childhood experiences. "Someday I will tell you more about my wanting to go to America. We never know what awaits us or how the decisions we make will change our lives. I never dreamed when I was a little boy of ever leaving England. Now, America will always be my home. There is untold wealth here for me and for you if it's what you want and this just may be where you should be. Give it some thought and prayer. God will show you his Divine Will."

When they arrived at the orphanage, there were no children playing in the yard as before. The house looked the same as Albert remembered, though the yard was much larger and had a wrought iron fence around it. Two women were sitting at a table in the shade having tea when Albert and his sons closed the gate behind them. "Hi, Mother," he said walking towards them. Lady Abigail and Margaret were startled at the sound of his voice. They had not seen them walk up.

His mother tried to stand but had to sit back down. She looked as though she was going to faint. Albert ran and steadied her so she would not fall. "Mother, it's your son, Albert. I am so sorry I startled you."

Both women looked at him and could not speak. His mother just pointed at him.

"Mother, me and my sons arrived late yesterday. I had no way to let you know we were coming." She reached out to him and he took her hand and lifted her up.

"Albert, I would not have known you had I met you on the street. You are so big, Son, and handsome. Did you say these are your sons?" she asked inquiringly.

"My adopted sons, Mother. If we may join you, I will tell you anything you want to know."

Margaret volunteered to go and get more tea and cookies. The questions from Abigail were endless so they talked for hours while Margaret showed Phillip and Bo around the orphanage, introducing them to the staff and all the children.

"Are you real Indians from America?" the children wanted to know.

"Our mothers were Indian and our fathers were white; that makes us half and half I would say," Bo told them, not wanting to explain his father was also mostly Indian.

"What kind of leg do you have?" one little boy asked looking at Bo's wooden leg.

"A doctor had to cut part of my leg off when I got hurt in an accident. The lower part is made of wood." He showed them how he could take it off and strap it back on, also showing them it did not slow him down. He ran a short distance and ran back doing the flip Bogie had taught him.

All the children, including the girls, were spellbound at his demonstration, wishing they could do those things.

"I bet you can learn," Bo said, "but it takes a lot of hard work."

The staff was also amazed when they found out Bo taught school in Denver, and also to the Indians.

The day passed quickly and Albert and his sons had to promise they would come back soon. Abigail wanted to hear more of Albert's life in America, and the children wanted to learn more about the Indians and how they lived in villages.

Phillip spent the next two days showing his grandsons the castle while Albert and Lord Anderson shared their experiences of the last few years.

"I'm glad Father was able to handle things for you, sir. I feel bad I left when you needed me."

"This is not the kind of life you are cut out for, Albert. We are all different. The things you have accomplished are as important as working for me. If I were a few years younger, I would go see for myself your America. I just wish I could have known Molly. She sounds a lot like my dear Eleanor."

The next two months passed quickly. They had all gone to London. Young Phillip and Bo could hardly believe the huge buildings and the number of people. It was a different world to them. Bo said he could not live in a place like London, though Phillip felt the opposite. "There is so much to do and so many things to see. I could live here forever."

Albert was a little concerned about the way Phillip was affected by the big city. Lord Anderson and Albert decided to return to their hotel and let the boys continue their tour of

London.

"You know, Albert, young Phillip is a rightful heir to the Anderson holdings, and he seems to fit in these surroundings. Have you considered a higher education for him? He is a bright lad and this may be where he belongs."

Albert did not answer for a while. *He remembered how he felt when his Uncle Bogie talked about America. How he was drawn to a place he had never seen. Did he have a right to deny Phillip his feelings if this is where he wants to live?*

"Grandfather, what would you think if Phillip really wanted to stay here and go to school?"

"I want what is best for him. Ask and give him time to make up his own mind. If this is what he wants, he will have the best education available."

Young Phillip could not stop talking about things and places he saw. There was no doubt in Albert's mind the boy belonged here where his father grew up and to be known as an Anderson, not be denied like his father.

"Son, what if you had the chance to stay here and go to school, would you stay?"

It was as if Phillip lost his voice. He certainly had not thought of living here, not in such a wonderful place as England. Then the reality of it struck him, of leaving Papa, Bo, and America.

"Don't make a decision now, Son. We won't be leaving for a while. Just think about it."

Thinking about it consumed the rest of his time in London. His life would never be the same no matter what he decided to do. *Could he give up Papa and Bo? The mountain where Mama was buried? Would the new wear off and not be able to go back home to America?*

When they returned to the castle, Phillip asked Albert what he should do. "Son, I know this is a hard decision. It would be for me. I cannot tell you what to do. Sometimes, when a child of God has something this hard placed on them, they need to go off by themselves and talk to the Lord. Why don't you and Bo go to the little house where your father lived? There is nothing there to distract you and maybe you can figure this out."

He agreed to this, though he wanted to do it by himself. Albert and his son walked the mile or so without much talking, each with his own thoughts. The cabin was just as Bogie had left it except for the dust and spider webs. They brought enough food and water for a few days and Albert helped Phillip clean and ready the cabin.

"If you are not back in three days, I will come and check on you, Son. There is nothing around to bother you, so don't be afraid."

"I won't be scared, Papa. I'm afraid I will make the wrong decision. I really want to stay, but I want to be with you also. How will I know?"

"Talk to God, Son, and I will too. You will know what is best."

"Papa, tell me again about my real father. I know this cabin was where he lived and you didn't know he even existed until you met him here by accident. What was he like?"

"Your father was as good a man as I ever met. I've told you the story of how his mother was taken advantage of by his real father who was my great grandfather. He promised to marry her but married someone else. Bogie was six months old when my grandfather was born. They grew up and played together as boys but he was denied the Anderson name, which has now been corrected. His name, along with yours is recorded in the Anderson archives, but don't ever forget you also have an Indian heritage on your mother's side, Singing Dove, the daughter of a Ute chief."

They talked a long time about how Phillip's life might be if he were to stay here in England and if he were to go back to America.

"You know I have been called by God to preach the Gospel and will soon have to leave here and go back. I will miss you if your decision is to stay, but I will understand. Do what you think is right and we will abide by what you decide."

Albert left Phillip alone knowing his son would do a lot of soul searching before he reached a decision.

Phillip sat on the front porch until long after dark in an old rocking chair which had seen better days. He wondered how many times his father must have sat in this same chair. Was he bitter about how his father rejected him and his mother? How would he feel now knowing Bogie was reinstated to his rightful place and that he may one day have his picture placed alongside the other Andersons? The scripture he remembered his papa often saying, "Be sure your sins will find you out," Phillip quoted out loud. Later in the night, he prayed for God to give him a sign showing him what to do.

Phillip never slept past sunup, though the sun was shining brightly the next morning when he awoke. He had been tired when he went to bed, but now he felt refreshed and ready for the day. The sun shone through a small window and where it lit the wall across the room, a picture of a little boy was hanging. Phillip threw the covers aside and went to look more closely at the picture. There was no writing to tell who it might be. "Sometimes the identification is on the back," he said. He took the cardboard out to see if anything was on the back. There was a one-page letter behind the picture and *Bogie - 6 years old* written on the back. Phillip carefully unfolded the letter and read.

My dearest love, forgive me for what I have done to you and my son. I have no acceptable excuse, yet I must try and explain. I was not married when I fell in love with you. Lucy, my wife, and I were pledged to each other by our parents years ago. Neither of us wanted this marriage. She loved someone else and I loved you. We were forced to do this and I was too weak to fight back. We were married when I found out you were going to have my child. I was glad and also sad. Lucy and I are also going to have a child

and if you will agree to let us raise your child,
we will say we had twins. You can come and help
raise them both. This, I know, is a lie, but I
cannot think of anything else. Lucy knows about
you and will agree to it. I love you.

Phillip sat on the side of the bed and read the letter the second time and took a closer look at his father's picture. "Did you know about this, Father? Your father did love you and Grandmother. He must have lived a miserable life not being able to call you his son. I have to show this to Papa."

Phillip knew he received his answer from the Lord. He would stay here and get his education and do his best to work and care for the Anderson holdings. He made the bed and placed the old rocking chair in the house. "I will be back often and rock in my father's chair," he commented.

With the picture of Bogie in one hand and the letter in the other, Phillip raced towards the castle to share what God had revealed to him. The long-ago mystery was brought to light.

The three generations of Anderson men read the letter. "It was Bogie's mother who didn't want to share her son with another woman," Lord Anderson declared.

"I can understand her not wanting to live with such a lie. The thing which bothered him most was the grief it caused his mother," Albert stated. "Knowing he was an Anderson was good enough for him. He could care less about not having a title."

After discussing the letter, Phillip said he wanted to stay in England, get an education, and work for the family. "This is what I believe my parents would want me to do. Papa, do you think it is wrong to want this for myself?"

"No, Son, I believe you are making the right decision, and I will be praying for you."

The die was cast. Phillip Anderson and his descendants would one day control the huge Anderson fortune, but for now, he had to grow up and get an education.

Albert and Bo stayed another three months before going back to America. They delayed leaving as long as possible to see if Phillip really wanted to stay. Then deciding this was destined to be, they sadly said their good-byes and departed. Leaving part of their family and Dap, Albert's beloved horse his grandfather gave him on his sixteenth birthday. "You are getting too old to make another long voyage, my friend. This is where you belong."

Their return voyage by ship took them longer because they wanted to see more of the southern part of America. Their route took them down the eastern coast, around the tip of Florida and into the Gulf of Mexico. They departed the ship at New Orleans and continued their journey on a paddle wheeler up the Mississippi River to St. Louis. From there, a coach brought them to Denver, the last leg of their travels.

"It has been a long and hard trip, Son," Albert said after stiffly stepping out of the coach.

Their plans were to buy a couple of horses, get some supplies and go to their cabin on the mountain. When they entered Carl's Mercantile, the first person they saw was Robert, the young preacher.

"Am I glad to see you two? We expected you back three months ago."

"We are just as glad to be back, Robert. How is everyone?"

"Nothing has changed, pastor. Your house is waiting for you. We cleaned it up a while back hoping you would stay here in town and preach for us again."

"Robert, you are the pastor now. We are here to buy a few things and go to the cabin on the mountain for the winter. Come spring, we will see you."

Robert gave the list for supplies to his younger brother to gather up and went to tell his father that Pastor Albert had returned. Before long, the whole town knew the news and the store was crowded with members of the church where Albert once pastored. They tried to get him to wait till spring before going up the mountain, but his mind was made up.

"We will see you when the snow melts," he said as he and Bo left on their new horses, leading a pack horse loaded with supplies.

CHAPTER SEVENTEEN

It took them almost four days to make the trip up the mountain. The last two days, snow slowed them down to a slow-moving pace. When they were in sight of the cabin, smoke curled out of the chimney.

"I wonder if Runner is waiting for us to come home like before?"

"I hardly think so, Son. He is too superstitious about Indians on the mountain in the wintertime. They believe the spirits of the Old Ones would be angry with them."

They tied the horses to the hitch rail in front of the cabin and Albert knocked on the door.

"Thought you'd come to your senses little gal when you got cold and hungry," someone said as the latch turned. "I got a good mind..." He did not finish what he was saying when he saw Albert and Bo standing there.

"What do you have in mind to do?" Albert asked jerking the door out of the man's hand.

"We don't cater to strangers, mister."

"I believe you are the stranger. This happens to be my house and I'll have an explanation as to why you are here."

The big burly man was caught completely off guard. Albert shoved him back into the house causing him to trip over a chair.

"I will ask you one more time. What do you have a mind to do?"

"Ah, I didn't mean anything. My wife's mad at me and is staying in the barn."

Albert asked Bo if he would take the horses to the barn and

see about the woman while he talked to their intruder. He told the man, who said his name was Ed, to get up off the floor and make clear what he was doing there.

Ed explained that he and his wife came across the cabin two weeks ago and it looked deserted. "We thought to stay a few days and move on when the weather got better, meant no harm, mister."

"Why are you in the warm cabin burning my firewood and she is out in the cold barn?"

"We just had a little spat. She ain't been in the barn but a little while."

When Bo lifted the latch on the barn door, it was locked on the inside. He pounded on the door and told whoever was inside to open up.

"You crazy old man, just try and come in here and I'll brain you with a club."

Bo said he was not who she thought he was that he and his father owned this place and no harm would come to her. He just wanted to tend his horses and find out what was going on. Bo waited a minute or two before hearing the latch being lifted. Expecting to see an older woman, he was surprised seeing a girl standing before him.

"I come to talk to your mother. The man in the house said his wife is staying in the barn."

"He's my stepfather. He is the reason I am here in the barn. My mother left and now he says I will have to take her place, the crazy old goat."

"What is your name and how long have you been locked up in this barn?"

"My name is Nancy and I don't know how long I've been in here, several days maybe."

Bo could not believe what he was hearing. Nancy had been living on horse feed and apples and drinking water from the creek at night. The tact room, once used for a bedroom, still had a bed in it. Bo's heart went out to her. She had not had a change of clothes or a good meal for days. Her long honey-colored hair was in knots. She had the largest and prettiest blue eyes he had ever seen.

"Can you help me, mister?"

"I can. My father and I will not let him near you. Wait just one minute until I tend my horses."

Nancy stayed close to Bo while tending the horses. He reached out for Nancy's hand. "Come with me. Don't be afraid. We will take care of you."

She hesitated for just a moment then placed her small hand in Bo's.

"Thank you, sir," she said. Her bright blue eyes seemed to sparkle.

Fear showed on the face of her stepfather when they entered the room. He started to say something and move towards Nancy and Albert shoved him back in his chair. There was a shocked look on Albert's face when he saw the little girl.

"Who do we have here, Bo? Where is this man's wife?"

"This is Nancy. She locked herself in the barn to get away from this man. He told her she had to be his wife since her mother left him. She is cold and hungry, Father. Let her tell you what she has been doing for God knows how many days."

Bo set about preparing a meal. First, he had to wash all the dishes, pots and everything else because of the dried food caked on them. Nancy started crying as she told Albert the horrid story of how her stepfather treated her and her mother.

"I don't believe my mother left me here with him. I don't know what, but I think he done something bad to her."

Albert knelt down and hugged her, wiping her tears away. Bo could hardly keep from crying himself. *How can a grown man treat a little girl like this?* he thought.

Soon the aroma of vegetable stew filled the cabin. A bowl was given to Nancy first and they watched as she gulped it down. She ate her second helping slower. When some was offered to Ed, he said he was not hungry.

"What are we going to do about this, Father?" Bo asked.

"There are a few more things I want to know before

deciding what we should do. Heat some water so Nancy can take a bath while us men go out to the barn and talk."

Bo opened the trunk and got out some of Phillip's clothes for Nancy and told her to take her time, they would be a while talking to Ed.

"We don't need to talk anymore, Father. Let's just hang him and get it over with like we did the other man," Bo said.

"Maybe it would be the thing to do, Son, but the other man didn't tell us the truth. Ed looks like he will. If he doesn't, we will do it your way."

Ed started pleading and begging for his life, even getting on his knees. "What do you want to know? I swear I will tell the truth."

"What did you do with Nancy's mother?" Albert asked. "I'll know if you are lying, Ed."

"I killed her. It was an accident. Two weeks ago, when we found this cabin, I told her to hurry up and build a fire and cook something. She refused because it wasn't our food. I just slapped her easy like and she hit her head on the corner of the table. I swear it was an accident. I hate I done it."

"Where is her body, Ed, and did Nancy see this accident?"

"She was in the barn. Her mama is in the tunnel behind the house. I never got around to burying her."

"And what about Nancy? Was she going to be your wife and next victim?"

"I was joking with her. She's just a kid."

Nancy was told the horrid news about her mother and all she could say was she knew that her mother would never leave her with this crazy man.

"I can't cry anymore. I'm just so sad for Mama."

Albert placed horse hobbles on Ed and tied him with a rope to a post in the barn.

"We will bury your mother in the morning and then bring Ed back to Denver where he will stand trial for murder. Then we will find you a home," Albert promised Nancy.

Albert cooked breakfast the next morning and brought some

to Ed. He had hanged himself during the night, afraid something worse would happen to him.

Lord, what makes a man like Ed? Did he never know about you? What makes their heart so hard and their mind so warped? If I had turned him loose, he would be alive now. Did I do wrong or would he have killed someone else? Albert thought to himself.

Albert spent an hour praying, searching his soul for answers.

Another reason for me to preach the Word of God. I have to go where these kinds of people are. They don't go to church, so I have to go where they are. "Thank you, Heavenly Father, for revealing this to me."

Two graves were dug in the morning. Nancy's mother was buried near Molly and Ed across the meadow from the cabin. A prayer was said for both and Nancy cried for both.

"I don't understand why he was so mean, not only to my mother and me, but to everyone, especially women," Nancy commented, tears running down her cheeks.

"There are some things we will never understand," Bo said trying to console her. "One thing is for sure, if we accept God into our life, we see things differently."

The afternoon was spent cleaning the cabin and washing sheets and blankets. Next morning, Albert asked Nancy if she had any family she would like to live with. She knew of no one and asked if she could live with them.

Albert knew this would be impossible because of the type of ministry he was led to do. He and Bo, if he wanted to, would travel the back roads to out-of-the-way places where people had no churches. Some of these places included mining towns where corruption ran rampant and not many preachers ventured; and, Indian villages where God was not heard of. These would not be places for a girl of Nancy's age or a woman of any age.

"I am a preacher, Nancy. Until a few months ago, I pastored a church in Denver. Now, I am called to travel to places no moral or upstanding person would normally go. People like Ed live there and they need to hear the Word of God as much as anyone else.

I know families in Denver who would love to have a sweet girl like you live with them. You can go to school and church and make lots of friends. You have been dragged around from place to place never being able to do these things. With us, your life would be in danger at all times, never knowing what could happen next."

Nancy was downcast and heartbroken at first until she realized what Albert said was true. *I never had a friend before, never went to church or a real school,* she pondered. She then became excited and started asking questions about these things Albert spoke of.

"Will there be a family with a lot of children and a girl my age?"

"Tomorrow our journey to Denver will begin and we will see what we can do about finding you a new family."

Going down the mountain was quicker than going up. They passed through small mining camps which were not there six months before. New deep rutted roads led off the main mountain road with names of towns like New Hope, High Dollar, and Silver Town.

"There are people all over this mountain, Bo. Our work of preaching the gospel to them won't be easy, but it never has been. God will give us what we need to do the job."

Denver was no longer a town; it was a city bursting at the seams. A huge three-story building named Denver Imports towered above the other buildings. Buggies and wagons of all sizes and makes jammed the streets and people were everywhere. They made their way to Carl's store, which also had been added onto. He was in his office talking to three different salesmen who were trying to get him to handle their product. He politely told them to wait in the store while he talked to his pastor.

Albert explained the situation and asked Carl if he could help them.

"No problem there, pastor. Nancy can stay with us until we

find a family she likes. My wife and I would love to have her live with us on a permanent basis, but we have no girls. She will have all the time she needs to find her a family."

Albert also told Carl what his new ministry would be and asked that he and the church pray for him and Bo. He promised Nancy they would check on her when they were in the vicinity. She said she would also pray for them and not to worry about her. When they came again, they could visit her in her new home. She kissed them on the cheek and thanked them for all their help.

Albert and Bo headed back up the mountain. Their plan was to visit as many mining towns as possible before hard winter set in. Then they would spend the remainder of the winter in the Ute village with Bo's people.

Three days travel brought them to where several men were living in tents and make-shift rooms. Trenches were dug in a small square and poles set vertically in them tied together with strips of leather. Other poles were placed on top close together and covered with dirt. When they found their visitors were there to tell them about God, they were not interested. Winter supplies was what they wanted, nothing else.

The next two little settlements were the same. No one wanted to hear preaching. A decision was made to wait till spring and try mining settlements. Now they would go where the Indians would be more receptive than the white people.

The whole Ute village was in the process of preparing freshly killed meat for the winter when they arrived.

"Good to see you again, White Brother," Runner said shaking Albert's hand. "See how we have been blessed with a good supply of winter food?"

Everyone in the village graciously received Albert and Bo. The older boys pastured the horses next to the river. Their packs were placed in the large teepee that once belonged to Bo's father, Chief White Wolf.

"We have to talk of Bible things," Runner said.

"And what things are you talking about?" Albert asked.

Runner wanted to know about being baptized. He had read when one is saved, next comes the baptism.

"You are absolutely right. After a person accepts Christ he then should be baptized."

"We have been reading the Bible you gave us the last time you were here and several of us accepts Christ, the Son of God, as our Lord. Can you and Bo do this for us?"

"The river is a might cold this time of year, but it won't take long to baptize you."

The whole village walked the short distance to the river and eight souls were baptized in the name of the Father, the Son and the Holy Ghost. Then a celebration was held in the evening in honor of the baptism and the successful hunt for their winter meat.

"There is much we don't understand. You will have to teach us so we will know."

Albert said they had the rest of the winter to read and discuss the bible.

When Albert and Bo lay in their blankets, Albert said, "This is too good to be true. Runner not only reads the whole Bible to their village, he traveled to the Comanche village of Red Cloud where his wife is from and told them about the Christian Faith. What a preacher he is going to make."

For two weeks, those who wanted to take part in the reading and discussion of the Bible did so, and three more made a profession of faith and were baptized. Several trips were also made during the winter to the Comanche village to preach to them.

The last visit, Albert, Bo, and Runner were sitting and talking with Red Cloud in his teepee when he said, "Your talking about the white man's God is upsetting the village. Most of our people trust you, Preacher Albert. They think you are a good man, being white, but there are other white men we don't trust. They come in many wagons across our hunting grounds and slaughter everything they see. There are stories told of them killing our people in other places. If true, there will be war and I don't want to see you in the middle of it. I can see you only want to help, but we have worshipped our way ever since we existed and most of us will not change our custom. It is best you do not come back for a while. If it makes you feel better, I believe in your Jesus and have for many years. Your friend, Bogie, told me about him and I have believed in him ever since. Now, you go back to our friends, the Utes. I will one day come and see you and we will talk more about God."

Albert knew there was the beginning of unrest between the Indians and the whites. He also knew there would soon be wholesale killing from both sides.

"If there is war, we don't have a chance to survive," Bo said on their way back to their village. "The Indians don't know how many whites there are and neither do they have the powerful guns of the white people. God help us if there is a war."

That winter, if one had counted the wagon trains camped east of the Rocky Mountains waiting for the snow to melt so they could continue their journey west, they would have seen that there were forty-some trains camped out and twenty more on the way. As Red Cloud said, hundreds of buffalo, deer and elk were killed to feed the people. There would certainly be war in the near future.

Albert and Bo stayed with the Utes the rest of the winter leaving for Denver when the grass began to green up.

They just thought the streets were crowded when they left the previous fall. Twice as many people were in and outside the city. Tempers flared over nothing. Some were seeking food, which was hard to find, and if you did, the prices were so high most did not have the money. If you could find an egg, it would cost twenty dollars or more. Many were trying to get to Oregon and others just wanted mining equipment. Gold and silver strikes were found in abundance in the mountains, or so they heard.

Carl had locked the door to his store. A sign said 'Out of Business'. When Albert knocked, he was motioned to the back.

"The people have gone completely mad," he said as he

hurriedly ushered Albert and Bo in the back door. "It has been this way for two months. I have nothing to sell and can't get a thing. Thank goodness my wife convinced me to hold back enough food and things for us or we would be like all of them crazies out there."

Nancy was the first one they saw when they entered the house part of the building. They were astonished when she walked out of her room. She did not look like the little girl they left behind. Good healthy food and helping in the store in her spare time had made a different person of her. She was much more mature and had a very beautiful smile. She ran and kissed each of them and said, "Welcome to my new home and family." When Bo could talk, he said he thought she wanted a family with girls.

"I thought I did but I found this was what I needed. I am in a family who loves and cares for me and I them. This is the best place ever. Thank you for bringing me here."

"Nancy is the daughter we never had and always wanted. We thank you for bringing her to us," Carl said.

Nancy wanted to know where they were going next after finding out they spent the winter with the Indians.

"We will try the mining towns again," Albert said. "Just because things didn't work before don't mean they won't now. I feel just as strong about this ministry as I did when Molly and I started one here in Denver years ago. We will be dealing with a different type people than we have here, but they also need to hear the Word of God."

Carl suggested they go to Agate Springs northwest of Denver. The word is it is the fastest growing town in Colorado. Most every claim up there has hit pay dirt.

CHAPTER EIGHTEEN

The trip up the mountain this time was a little different than before. Many more people, some going to seek their fortune and some sick and tired of hunting for something they could not find. One of the men they met on his way down told them not to waste their time. "All of the good places have already been claimed," he said. "If you are lucky enough to find a nugget, someone will take it away from you dead or alive, makes them no difference."

"We're going to tell them about the Lord, not to hunt gold."

"Take my advice and save yourself some trouble. Don't even try something so foolish. The only thing they want to hear is the sound of whiskey being poured in a glass. You'll be sorry," were the last words they heard him yell as he hurried down the road.

"This must be the town we are looking for," Bo said with a big smile.

They could hear the people before they saw them. Several shots were fired and someone was yelling at the top of his voice, "I hit the mother lode. Drinks are on me."

As they passed two tents still under construction, Albert pointed to a man across the street watching them. "I know that man."

The man turned and walked back into the building, the only wooden structure on the far end of town. A large sign across the front read, 'Wild Horse Saloon'.

Agate Springs was the largest mining town in this part of Colorado. Almost a year earlier, a hunter found a four-pound gold nugget in the stream. When the news got out, there was a scramble to file claims on every inch along the creek.

Albert and Bo looked the settlement over, riding the length of the one main street.

"I counted four saloons but not one church," Bo exclaimed when they turned and headed back through town. They stopped in front of the Wild Horse Saloon to Bo's dismay. "Are we going in there?" he asked.

"I need to talk to the man we saw a few minutes ago. He may be able to help us."

Albert was in front of Bo when they went through the swinging doors. The man they were looking for was sitting at a table in back of the crowded room. They made their way to where he was sitting and he nodded his head for them to sit.

"Here to burn my business and run me out of town again?" he asked, thumbing through a deck of cards, not looking at Albert.

"If you remember correctly, Mr. Smith, it was your hired hoodlums who tried to run me out of Denver. As for burning your business, I would say the citizens were tired of the way you treated their preachers. Anyway, that was a long time ago. I'm here to ask for your help."

Smith set his cards aside and asked Albert and Bo to be seated, looking bewildered.

"You still preaching or looking to get rich like everyone else?"

"This is my son, Bo, and we are still preaching the Word of God."

"And you want me to build you a church here in Agate Springs?"

"The church building can come later. What I want now is a place to preach this Sunday."

Smith could not believe what he heard. He chuckled and shook his head. "Preacher, there is not a vacant place in town. I watched you ride through. Did you see any place?"

"Here, in your saloon, on Sunday morning. You can stop

selling liquor for an hour, can't you?"

"I don't believe you, preacher. You asking to use what you call a house of sin to preach in?"

"Yep, it's what I'm asking, for one hour from eleven to twelve Sunday morning."

Smith pondered the request for a while. "This just may be good for business, preacher. I'm willing to give it a try. How much is this going to cost me?"

"Nothing at first. Later on, it could cost you some of your customers."

Smith laughed again and kept saying, "This is a novel idea. Preaching in my saloon. OK. This is Friday. It will give us today and tomorrow, preacher, to gather a crowd for Sunday. I'll spread the word. You get ready to preach it."

Albert and Bo camped on the edge of town and placed a little sign next to the road pointing to their campsite. The sign read, 'Albert and Bo Anderson Circuit Evangelists'. Smith installed a large banner under his Wild Horse Saloon sign advertising 'Preaching here Sunday, 11:00 am till'. Many came and talked to Albert and Bo about having church on Sunday in a saloon. Some were glad and others thought it better if they moved on.

The Wild Horse Saloon was packed Sunday morning when it was time for preaching. Several rough-looking miners standing at the bar commenced making fun of the preacher and his peg legged Indian dressed in mountain men clothes. Smith ordered them to leave their drinks on the bar and sit down or get out. They started to argue with Smith until two men with shotguns convinced them to do as they were told.

Albert started his message with, "We won't take much of your time today and we appreciate you coming this morning to the first church service in Agate Springs. My son and I have lived in these mountains for many years and the kind of clothes we wear are the best for living in the wilderness. Some of you, I would say, were brought up in church and others may have never heard the gospel preached. I know this may seem an odd place to have a service for the Lord. Smith is gracious enough to let us use his building to share the Word of God with you.

I am not going to tell you drinking, gambling and other vices are wrong. You already know the answer. This is not the first time I have been in a mining town and not the first time to be in such places which harbor all sorts of evil.

What I want to share with you this morning is Jesus Christ, the Son of God. He offers much more than one can ever find in a place like this. You are hoping to find gold or silver, thinking it will give you what you are looking for, but it won't. The rich people of this world are still looking for something to satisfy them. Peace of mind, happiness, satisfaction, cannot be dug from the ground, though they can be found here, even in Agate Springs, if you search in the right place. Jesus is the only source where you can truly find these things and much, much more. Don't fool yourself into thinking differently. I'll not take any more of your time this morning. If you truly want the things we talked about, come see me and my son in our camp just east of town, and we will introduce you to the one who can help you."

Albert spoke for no more than ten minutes, his audience listening to every word. They were expecting to hear a hellfire and brimstone sermon condemning them to a devil's hell. As He and Bo walked across the room, not a word was spoken, even from the rowdy miners. When the double doors closed behind them, they heard Smith say, "The first round is on the house, men."

Three tall bearded men heard Albert speak and were waiting for him outside.

"Are you the same Albert Anderson who was the pastor of a church in Denver?"

"Yes, I did at one time pastor in Denver."

"We never met you though we heard a lot of good things about you. What was said here this morning is the same as we believe. We have settled in a valley, six miles west of here. There are nine families in all. Our wives and children are with us and we are in need of someone to help lead us in a spiritual way. We come from Ohio and our pastor got deathly ill halfway here and had to go back. None of us know enough to take on the duty of preaching. Will you help us?"

Albert agreed to go and see what could be done, though for the next few Sundays, he felt obliged to preach here in Agate Springs. "Tomorrow we will come to your valley. Preaching can be done any day of the week."

Others came in the afternoon and asked if it would be possible to build a small church here where they were camping. They would build a building if he would preach for them.

"Let us make it a matter of prayer. If God is in it, it will happen."

As they sat outside their tent and listened to the revelry sounds coming from town, Bo asked if this place would ever be like Denver.

"I doubt it, Son. Like most boomtowns, the gold will play out and the people will leave and go to the next place where a nugget is found. There is more hope for the valley where we go tomorrow. There is no law and order here and most don't want any. Those men who talked to us about preaching to their families have a better chance to build a real town. They want to have God in their lives and that is what will make the difference. First, they want a church then a school. Law and order is already there. You watch and see. Agate Springs is a good representation of a lost and dying world while those few people in the next valley over represent the righteousness of God. They will struggle, but they will make it."

Mid-morning the next day, the two men topped out on a rise and were looking down on a beautiful valley. They saw several cabins with smoke curling from chimneys and plots of ground that had been recently plowed.

"This looks a lot like our place on the mountain," Bo commented.

The rutted road wound back and forth to the bottom where the ground leveled off. The first of the cabins they came to was the largest and it looked like most of the settlers were there waiting for something. The spokesman they talked to the day before came forward and said this was not a good time for them to be here. "We are expecting trouble from the Indians. Yesterday while we were talking to you, they came here and made signs for us to leave. The best our people could understand is they were coming back today."

"Have you had trouble in the past with them?" Albert asked.

"No, we have seen a few from time to time, but never have they even talked to us in the three years we have been here."

Albert could definitely tell they were upset, especially the women. The children, except two older boys, were made to stay inside. The other nine cabins could be seen from where they were. Built of large logs and stone, Albert knew they were built to last.

"Maybe they were trying to frighten you into moving," Bo said trying to console them, knowing if the Indians told them to leave, they meant just what they said.

He also knew the settlers were here to stay even if they had to fight. The unrest between the Indians and the whites was growing at an alarming rate. He was three quarters Indian and felt sorry for them because in the long run, they did not have a chance if it came to war.

Mid-afternoon when it looked like the trouble was over for the day, one of the men cried out, "Oh my God!"

There must have been a hundred Indians coming towards them. The nine men and the two older boys instantly were armed with rifles and side arms.

"Whatever you do, don't shoot," Albert instructed. "They intend to talk first. Let's give them a chance."

"Papa, if my eyes don't deceive me, I see Chief Red Cloud of the Comanche with other chiefs, whom I don't recognize."

"You are right, Son. Let's go try and talk to them."

Albert stood his rifle against the wall and told three of the men to do the same.

They hesitated and then did as they were told. As they walked towards the Indians, Red Cloud and two more of the chiefs dismounted and met them half way.

"What are you doing here, Albert Anderson?" Red Cloud asked.

"I am here preaching to my friends Why are you so far away from your village?"

"These are my Cheyenne brothers. They live north of here and the Comanche live south. This is neutral ground. When they have trouble, we help them. If we have trouble, they do the same."

"Which of you are having trouble today? Bo and I will help you both."

This question caused Red Cloud to think. Neither Comanche nor Cheyenne claimed this valley. He turned to the other chiefs and said something Albert did not understand.

"We will talk, Albert Anderson. You bring your three friends and Bo. We have much to talk about."

Albert informed the three settlers not to say anything unless asked a question.

A place under a huge ponderosa pine was selected for their meeting. Albert and Bo were introduced to the chiefs and they to him.

"We have heard of you Albert Anderson. You live on the mountain in the wintertime with the spirits of the Old Ones. They say the spirits have accepted you. Do you have their power?"

"The Spirit of God gives me power. His Spirit lives within me at all times and is with me wherever I go. He is with me now."

"What are you to these people here living on our land?"

"I come here to tell them about my God just as I tell all people everywhere about him, not just white people, but Indians also. Ask this good friend of mine, Chief Red Cloud."

"He has already spoken of you and your son, Bo."

"It is good to know you great chiefs of the Cheyenne Nation. I would like to ask you to let these friends of mine be your friends also and live in this valley. They will not give you any trouble. I can speak for them. If you ever need their help they will help you the same as I."

"We will give you our decision before the sun leaves the sky."

The meeting was over. Albert, Bo and the settlers went to their homes to await the chief's decision. They knew if the Indians wanted them to leave, they had no choice. To try and resist would be futile.

Just before sundown, the chiefs rode their beautiful spotted ponies into the settlement. "We agree, you who are here now can stay and raise your families, but you cannot bring anyone else here to live. Every year the Cheyenne and Comanche will check on you. If you ever need our help, send someone. Albert Anderson's friends are our friends."

Then they turned to Albert. "Albert Anderson, you come to the Cheyenne village to the north. We will hear you speak about your God and his mighty Spirit of which you spoke."

"There you have it," Albert commented when all the Indians left the premises. "Their word is good. You will never have trouble with them as long as you do as they say."

"When you came here this morning, we said it was a bad time for you to be here. We have seen the power of God work here today, Reverend Anderson. Will you stay here and preach for us?"

"Not now. God has called me to be an evangelist, to go wherever he sends me. To towns, homes, Indian villages, anywhere there are people who need to hear the Gospel. I will preach here and in Agate Springs until the snows come, then I will go where I can travel to places on the plains."

The settlers had no more trouble with Indians; in fact, they were accepted by them and aided when there was a need. They built themselves a church and their first pastor was Bo Anderson. He led them as the Spirit of God led him, following in the footsteps of Albert.

There were those in Agate Springs Albert reached with the Gospel message. Lives were changed and Smith began to lose those as customers. Each Sunday, the crowds in the saloon increased, most came to hear him speak, not to indulge in drinking and gambling. Even Smith began to be moved by the Word of God.

Towards the end of summer, he followed Albert and Bo back to their campsite after Sunday's service. He said he wanted to talk to them about salvation.

"I don't understand exactly what being born again means," Smith said.

"In John 3:5-6, Jesus himself said, except a man be born of water and of the Spirit, he cannot enter into the kingdom of God. That which is born of the flesh is flesh; that which is born of the Spirit is spirit. This simply means when a person realizes he is without God in his life and wants more than anything to remedy this and ask God to come into his life, he is instantly, spiritually born again into the kingdom of God. This is what being saved means. It is an act of faith on our part and a work of the Holy Spirit on God's part. Christ made this all possible by his death and resurrection. Do you believe, Smith?"

"Yes, I believe. Now what do I do, preacher?"

"Read God's Word, pray for whatever is on your heart and follow the leadership of the Holy Spirit."

In the days following, Albert saw a drastic change in the life of Smith. The first thing he did was to dispose of all of the liquor and gambling devices in his saloon. A new sign replaced the saloon sign saying, 'First Church of Agate Springs'.

Some of his hard-core customers threatened him and went to another saloon. Others saw the change in his life and wanted what he had. Albert called him a "shining example". In the winter, he left the mining town when Albert and Bo left. Agate Springs lasted as long as the gold did. Like Albert predicted, one year later there was nothing there, just the spoils that man always leave behind.

Then Albert started what he called his circuit preaching in earnest. He and Bo headed south to the Ute village, then Fort Pueblo and Raton, west to Santa Fe, then as the weather warmed into spring, north to Grand Junction. They preached to as many as would listen; in towns, forts, at ranches and to prisoners in jails. The Rocky Mountains was where he felt closest to the Lord. The next year, he went north to Fort Casper in Wyoming, then east and south to Denver, an ever-growing city. Then, Bo decided to pastor the small settlement close to where Agate Springs use to be. Albert continued his circuit where the people were expecting him and he was welcome by all, both Indians and whites. Mostly he lived off the land. The mountains were his home; he knew their secrets hidden from most. Albert could find the paths which were used by people so long ago and now no longer detectable. His eyes were keen and his body hard and strong as steel. His beard and hair now white as new fallen snow, and as true to all the Anderson men, his hair only got thicker. Most of the time now he traveled on foot going places a horse could not go. The higher the peaks, the stronger his spirit became. There was an aura about him one could feel in his presence. The churches where he preached likened him to the apostle, Paul, going from place to place preaching the Gospel. When he was known to be in one of the larger cities, hundreds of people would flock to where he preached. He shared the Word of God to crowds or to one. "Everyone has a soul which is important to God and my job is to witness to him," he would say.

On one of his stops in Denver, there was a letter from his father. He had written several, though this was his first to receive. It was written four months earlier. It read,

Son, your grandfather has passed away. He loved you greatly and talked of you often acclaiming you the greatest of all the Andersons. Young Phillip is a man now and is most intelligent. His spare time, which is very little, is spent working with me taking care of family business. Your mother is well also.

Enclosed is a note from your grandfather.

Your Father, Phillip

My dear Grandson, I was hoping to see you one more time but it must not be in God's plan. I picture you in your mountain clothes, standing tall, with a Bible in one hand and your rifle in the other like in the story you told when you preached your first sermon. I would have loved to have been there. The pastor in our little town visits often here at the castle and I tell him about you. I spent most of my life without God. Oh, how foolish. Thank you for sharing Him with me. I am much of the time in bed now. My body is frail, though my mind is still as it always was, and I thank him. By the promises of God, I will see you in heaven."

Your Grandfather,
Albert Anderson,
Who loves you much

Tears were streaming down Albert's snowy white beard while he read the letter several times more. "Dear, dear, Grandfather. If it had not been for you asking me what I intended to do with my life, God only knows where I would be. It is I who should be thanking you."

Later the same day before he left Denver, he answered with another letter to his father. Intending to keep his family in England informed of his activities here in America.

Albert was a man born in England, though in all ways, he was a Mountain Man of the Rockies. Mile after mile, and year after year, he walked and preached, leading people to Christ, until he himself begin to tire. The strenuous climb through the mountains became slower and slower each year. Like his loving grandfather, his eyesight and mind were as sharp as ever, but the strength and hardness of his body began to diminish.

Carl, Albert's friend of so many years, had passed away and his youngest son with his wife, Nancy, now ran the store. He made an order for a month's worth of supplies to be brought to his cabin on the mountain and asked if someone would go and tell Preacher Bo to come and see him there. Nancy assured him Bo would get the message. He borrowed a horse to be brought back when the supplies were delivered and slowly made his way to the cabin on the mountain. The first thing he did was to go to where his loving wife, Molly, was buried and sat on the rock she sat on so many times.

He cried often now and tears filled his eyes. "My love, it won't be long now. We will be together soon. My journey has been a long one, but is most over now. I am ready to come home, dearest. My work here is finished."

He pulled a few weeds from her grave and led his horse into the barn, cleaned some cobwebs from the corners of the cabin and built a fire in the fireplace.

I wonder if we have any of that good English tea, he thought. Sure enough, on a shelf in a tightly closed jar, there was the tea. Slowly, the way Molly always sipped her tea, he drank two cups and went to bed.

CHAPTER NINETEEN

He was so very tired, he slept till almost noon. A pounding on the heavy oak door awakened him.

"The door is not locked," he yelled as he pulled on his trousers.

A tall man stood in the doorway and another young man beside him. The room was kind of dark and the light outside made it hard to see their faces clearly. When the man said "Papa?" Albert knew instantly who it was.

"Phillip, my son." Then as the two embraced each other, Albert said, "The Lord's timing is impeccable as it always is. Who is this with you, Son?"

"Papa, this is your grandson, Albert Anderson. I bring him here to meet you so you can talk to him about what it takes to be a minister for God. This is his calling, the same as yours. Son, this is your infamous grandfather who everyone within hundreds of miles knows."

Albert hugged his grandson and felt the same raw strength he used to have. He knew God had brought him here to do what he no longer could.

"The Lord giveth and the Lord taketh away, blessed be the name of the Lord."

"Not now, Grandfather, you can't go now. I need you to teach me and show me the way."

"God never calls one and not show him the way. He will teach you by his Word and experiences and empower you with his Spirit. I have found God is more than enough."

Albert opened the old trunk at the foot of the bed and took

out the sermon outlines Molly's grandfather had written over a hundred years before. Albert and others used them to study early in their ministry.

"These helped me and others, Son. They will be a help to you. Study them and don't ever get far away from the Word of God, which is a must if you want to succeed. Bo, who is your cousin, will be here shortly. He can also be a great help to you."

Albert wanted to know about England and his father. He had received a letter two years before informing him of his mother's death.

"Cousin Phillip retired one year ago, though he still helps me in the business, and I have another son who works with me. Albert, my son, has gone to the seminary for two years and felt the call to come here and preach. He wanted to have time with you, Papa."

They whiled the rest of the day away with Albert telling his grandson about his circuit ministry. "There is a great need to reach the ever-growing population moving into this part of the country. You will never run out of people to witness to."

The next day, Bo came galloping up to the hitch rail and was relieved when he saw Albert sitting on the rock beside Molly's grave. One look told him he was not well.

"Thanks for coming so soon, Son."

When Phillip and his son came out of the cabin, Bo was again surprised.

Albert took both Bo and Phillip by the hand and asked if they remembered the promise they made to him the day they buried Molly, and when his time came, they would bury him beside her. They both said they did remember their promise.

"The time is now, boys. I am so tired. Let us go into the house and rest." They led him into the cabin he loved so much and laid him in his bed, the same bed in which Molly nursed him back to health from his encounter with the mountain lion.

Both of his sons held his now feeble hands while his grandson prayed. Albert smiled at them and slowly closed his eyes. He was gone home.

Not only his sons grieved, but also all who heard of his death, Indians and white alike. Young Albert was not led to be an evangelist. He organized another church in the ever-growing city of Denver.

The circuit riding preaching died when Albert died.

The End

Photograph Copyright © 2011, Webster Miller

ABOUT THE AUTHOR

Donald Miller was born in a south Louisiana lumber mill settlement in the Atchafalaya Basin. He is a simple man of great spiritual conviction and wisdom. His first novel tells the fate of the families that struggled to build Lamb's Creek, a Tennessee community that spurned slavery and survived the bloodshed of the Civil War. Don lives in the hills of Tennessee with his wife, Dolores, and pup, Noggin, in an old tobacco barn they now call home.

For more information visit:

www.DonMillerWriter.com